ONE FINAL CHANCE

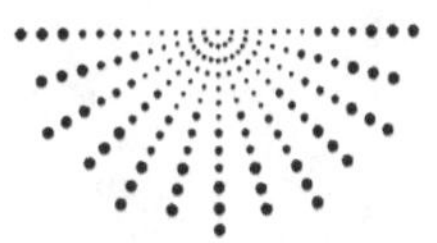

YM ZACHERY

A publication of Wild Dreams Publishing
Traralgon, Vic
© 2019 by YM Zachery
All rights reserved, including the right of reproduction in whole or in part in any form.
Wild Dreams Publishing is a registered trademark of Wild Dreams Publishing.
Manufactured in Australia.
All rights reserved.
Cover © Wild Dreams Publishing
Created with Vellum

❀ Created with Vellum

CHAPTER ONE

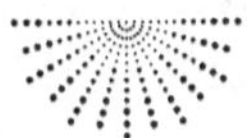

Paris looked at the computer and smiled to herself. The confirmation that she would be graduating from Seattle University with a Masters Degree in primary education meant that all of her dreams could finally come true. It also meant that the dream of employment and remaining in this country were finally being realised.

"You almost ready to get this party started?" Charmaine called from down the hall.

"Sure am." She yelled back. Charmaine was her best friend, room-mate and overall confidant. If it wasn't for Charmaine, Paris never would have made it here in America. Paris smiled to herself as she thought back on how she came to be living with her.

Charmaine was the same age as Paris, and they had become fast friends. The first week of her exchange, Charmaine had taken Paris under her wing and they had been inseparable ever since. Charmaine had already been working at the school for over a year as she had completed her internship there, not to mention Charmain had attended the school herself. That meant that she knew the ins and out of the school and that had helped Paris settle in quickly.

On top of that they had taken many road trips together. Charmaine had vowed that Paris was not going to return home; if she did that was not without having seen as much of America as she could. Not that Paris was complaining; she had always wanted to travel through the States.

Along with travelling and working together, the girls had bonded quickly and spent many a long night talking about their pasts, their futures and hopes and dreams, or just having fun. They *were* young after all. That was why Paris was happy that she was getting to share this moment with her best friend.

Paris took one last look at the confirmation on the screen before shutting it down and turning to the mirror. Her chestnut hair flowed down her back in waves, the diamonds in her heart-shaped, dangling earrings shone, and her black dress fit her like a glove. Yep, she was ready for another night out on the town to celebrate finishing her degree and the last step to freedom.

Freedom from her past and the freedom to create her future. Today was the first step to a new beginning, and it felt wonderful.

Flashbacks of her past started to try and make a comeback, piercing her happiness with stabs of darkness, but she would not allow that to happen tonight. Tonight was a celebration, not a time to dwell on things better left forgotten.

An impatient knock on the door brought her out of her sudden melancholy and she shook herself free. She had never been more grateful for her friend than she was in that moment. Paris reached down and grabbed her red and black heels.

"So, where are we headed?" She asked Charmaine as she met her at the front door.

Charmaine grinned her ecstasy-red lipstick grin. "Tonight, we are off to the Hyatt, my dear friend. I have a pal there who has booked us in for the night. We will hit the restaurant first and then head to Club 8 downstairs for some more drinks and dancing. Maybe if we're lucky, we will find us a date, or at least some men who will shout us some drinks."

Paris laughed. It was just like Charmaine to be on the hunt. This was the norm. They would go out once a month, drink, have fun and pick up a date for the night. They were always careful and never gave out their real names. It was their time to let their hair down and live life to the fullest. They didn't even have to take much money as their dates shouted them drinks and food most of the time.

'If men can do it, why can't we,' was always Charmaine's argument. And in a way she was right.

"Who are we tonight?" Paris asked as they walked outside and closed the door behind them, locking it as they went.

Paris knew she should feel more uncomfortable lying to people, but her childhood had taught her that lying was the norm, so when Charmaine had suggested it, Paris never thought twice about it.

"Tipany and Scarlet. We are sisters from Ohio on a weekend away." Charmaine laughed as she winked.

Paris chuckled because it could almost be true. Many had commented on how alike her and Charmaine looked.

"Alright, love it! Let's get this party on the road." Paris declared.

She was looking forward to tonight, it was going to be magical. For starters, they were not going to hit their normal local joints, instead they were going into the centre of town to one of the most upper-class clubs they could get into. On top of that, Paris was trying to forget about her last boyfriend, who was connected to a past she wanted to forget.

She had been with Liam for one year and was happily making plans with him for the future, when the truth of who and what he was came out. Liam of course hadn't meant for her to find out, the day she found the message on his phone a month ago, was the day it all became exposed. Paris' mind, of its own accord, wandered to the last time she had seen her family.

Sydney, Australia 2014

As Paris walked home, the evidence of her latest con in her bag, she thought about where her life was heading. For years she had done everything her father had asked her to do without question. But tonight's con just hadn't felt right. It hadn't since the day she turned eighteen, when she learnt just how far her father was willing to go to get what he wanted.

Normally Paris and her brothers ran the con together. They would hit the ritzy hotels in the Sydney town centre, looking for old, rich businessmen who were looking for the next big thing. Paris' older brother was a master at making himself look like a rich businessman, and he could talk any man into believing anything he said. Normally Paris went along to support her brother, pretending mostly to be his assistant. But as she grew older and more beautiful, her father had started to see a different potential in her.

That was how she ended up where she was tonight. One of the businessmen had hinted at wanting to spend the night with her, and her brother had agreed. When Paris tried to get the support of her father, he simply told her that she needed to start pulling her weight. She was told she was to do anything she could to make the man happy.

That was how she found herself in his hotel room that night.

Paris had been prepared to play the role; however, she had convinced the man to give her the cheque for the for the money first, made out to cash of course so that it could never be traced back to her family, and then she made a plan of her own.

Tears ran down her face as she walked the streets of Sydney, making her way to the train station. She felt cheap, but that was not what was bothering her. What was bothering her was the fact that she didn't know if she had killed a man or not. Pulling her coat closer around he, she wondered what she should do.

While the businessman hadn't been looking, Paris had slipped some sleeping pills into his wine, but the moment he'd had some, he had passed out. Paris had tried to wake him, but the man was unmoving. She thought about sticking around and finding out, she even considered calling an ambulance, but that would have brought her family into the light and they were always warned as kids never to do that.

That was how she'd ended up here, on a train making her way home. People were staring at her as though she was crazy, and she probably looked it with her mascara running down her face, her blonde hair falling out of its bun. An older woman looked at her with disgust in her eyes, probably picturing her as a working woman. And Paris couldn't even get angry at her, because if she had gone through with tonight, that was exactly what she would have been.

Ten minutes later, Paris was in Parramatta. She walked the ten minutes it took to get to their home and walked in.

The scene that greeted her was one she was used to. Her father and brothers sat at a table with her father's friends playing poker while her mother served them drinks and food. While her father was a con man, one thing she had to give him was that he loved her mother, no woman had ever been happier.

He worshiped the ground she walked on. That was why he turned to conning people in the first place. He wanted to give his queen everything, he just didn't want to work for it. And until that night she 'thought' he had felt the same way about her.

"Home already?"

Her older brother asked when she walked in.

"How did you go?" Her father asked, putting his cards down on the table.

Paris didn't answer him; she simply walked forward and placed the cheque on the table. It was the biggest amount they had ever conned out of someone.

"Oh, Princess you did well." Her father chimed giving her a hug.

It felt good to have his arms around her. He had always made her feel safe. It was the safe feeling that she was feeling that allowed the flood gates to her emotions open. Paris broke down crying into her father's arms. "I am so sorry Papa; I didn't mean to do it I promise."

She felt her father stiffen before he pushed her out at arm's length.

"Paris calm yourself and tell me what is going on."

The look in his eyes was one she had never seen before. She was a little worried, but his was her father, he would always protect her, or so she thought.

"What have you done?"

Paris explained what had happened in the hotel room. During her explanation most of the other occupants of the room had left. All that was remaining was her father, who was now pacing, her brothers, who were on the phone to all of their connections seeing if they could find out what had happened.

"Did you call the police?" Her father snapped. Paris took a step back.

"Off course not Papa, I know better." Paris watched as her father visibly relaxed.

"Good, now the cheque is in cash so they will not be able to trace that back to us."

"You didn't use your real name, did you?" One of her brothers

asked. Paris didn't answer him, she just gave him a look that told him she wasn't stupid.

"Okay I just got off the phone with my mate in the hospital and he said nothing has come in."

Her father laughed at that and patted her on the shoulder before sitting down. "See Princess nothing to worry about. And don't worry. Next time you will know what not to do."

Paris looked at her father in shock. How could he even think that she was going to do this? She'd had enough of this life. Tonight had taught her that she didn't want to spend her life on the run from cops, and she certainly didn't want to become what the old woman had thought she was.

"Look Papa, I was thinking, maybe it's time I..." Her father didn't let her finish. Standing up once more he towered over her.

"Now you listen to me Princess, and you listen well. You are part of this family, and as part of this family you will do as you're told. You are no better than the rest of us, you are my child and therefore 'this life' is in your DNA." He spat. Paris had never seen him look so angry. She wanted to argue with him, but right now she was actually scared of him.

"Now go upstairs and have a shower. Once you have finished, I want you to come back down here; we have much to discuss."

Paris had just left the kitchen and was heading up the stairs when her father's conversation to her brother caught her attention.

"I have a new plan. We are going to use Paris more. With the amount of money she conned from that businessman tonight without using her body, imagine how much we could get if we promise those lonely men a night with her."

Paris had expected her older brother to stand up for her, instead he laughed and agreed with his father. It was in that moment that she realised money was all they cared about. As long as the money kept coming in they didn't care how they got it, even if it meant selling her.

Tonight, she learnt, she was not like them.

She wanted out.

She wanted a life that didn't involve her selling her body or conning others out of their hard-earned money.

Walking into her bedroom Paris picked up the envelope that had just arrived yesterday. It contained the acceptance letter for her exchange program to the University of Seattle. Paris hadn't told her parents about it yet as she wasn't sure how they would handle it. And now she was thankful for that. Paris knew what she had to do. Closing and locking her door Paris got to work packing her bag and collecting the money she had saved for herself over the years, it would be the last of her father's dirty money that she would ever use. Later that night she snuck out of her parents' house, without leaving a note and disappeared into the night.

She found a place to lay low in another state and spent the next few months changing everything she could about herself. She legally changed her last name to Devon, got a new passport, dyed her hair to a chestnut colour, and applied for an exchange program at foreign universities. That was how she ended up in the States.

She had thought she was free and clear until a year ago when the truth about her boyfriend had come out.

SHE STILL COULDN'T BELIEVE that her father was still hiring people to try and control her. When Paris had first moved to America, she had hoped that she was far enough from his reach, but the moment Liam admitted who he was, Paris knew that no matter how far she ran her father would never let her go. When she had left, she took his most prized passion with her. It was not out of love that he chased her, it was out of pure greed.

Paris still remembered the night she decided to leave. It was the night she realised that her father did not love her.

He loved the money she brought in for him.

Shaking the cruel memories away, Paris once again forced herself to focus on tonight.

Tonight, Charmaine wasn't the only one who was going to be wild. For once, Paris was going to let her hair down. She was going to live in the moment. She was not going to be the voice of reason. For once she was going to be the rash one and she would deal with the reality of her decisions in the morning.

CHAPTER TWO

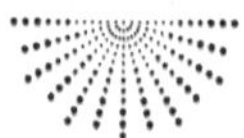

On opening her eyes, Paris saw that the clock on the side table read ten o'clock. The clock was not one she was used to seeing and it took a minute for her to remember where she was.

Paris laughed thinking that they were lucky that Charmaine had booked them in for two nights, otherwise they would have been staying whether they wanted to or not.

Paris thought about getting up, but the pounding in her head from the merriments of the night before had her closing her eyes once more. Lying as still as she could on the bed, so the pounding didn't increase, Paris listened to the quiet around her.

She was still considering whether she should get up, but as she continued listening she noted that Charmaine wasn't making any noise either, which meant she was still obviously sleeping, with that in mind, Paris decided to stay right where she was. It wasn't long before Paris once more drifted off into a headache induced slumber.

When Paris woke again, the clock this time read one in the afternoon, thankfully the pounding in her head had lessened to a dull ache. She could now get up and look at filling her stomach with some food.

Stretching her arms above her head, Paris realised she was still in the dress she had worn last night. An uneasy feeling started to crawl up her spine. Not only did she not remember climbing into bed, she didn't even remember making it up to their room. She had only been in here once – when they had arrived.

Charmaine had gone up and booked them in, Paris had needed to go to the toilet, she would have waited to get to the room, but she had been busting and her friend was too busy chatting up the bellhop. Paris left her friend there and Charmaine had texted her the room number. Once they had dumped their gear and gotten ready, both of them had made their way down to the restaurant, then down to the club.

That was when the party started. Paris remembered that they had gotten their drinks, found a table and started drinking. *But,* that was the last thing Paris remembered.

Looking up at the ceiling, she racked her brain to try and remember any moment after then, but she couldn't. The pounding was back, and a nauseous feeling started in the pit of her stomach. But this feeling was not from the alcohol, it was from the fact that she could not remember what happened last night.

God, she hoped Charmaine could fill in the blanks. Turning back on her back, she shook the bed blindly as she tried to rouse her friend.

"Char, are you awake? Please tell me you remember what happened last night."

The uneasy feeling continued to grow stronger when her friend didn't answer. Turning her head, Paris looked to see if her friend's eyes were even open, but she was facing away from Paris,

"Char?" Still no answer.

This time Paris tried, reaching out and shaking her.

Still no answer. It was in that moment that Paris realised that her friend was not moving. Paris tried to figure out what was going on. She moved her hand a little more firmly on Charmaine's arm, and pressed harder hoping the pressure would wake her, but all Paris felt was the cold clamminess of Charmaine's skin.

It was then Paris realised that her hand felt wet.

Why would Charmaine be wet?

Nothing about this morning was making any sense. Pulling her hand back, Paris brought it in front of her. Rubbing her fingers together she tried to get her mind to register what she was seeing. Paris wondered once again how much she had drunk last night. Never had she ever felt this hungover. Not only was she feeling headachy and ill, she was also feeling sluggish, like she was wading through water. It was then Paris noted that the confusion she was feeling was not due to the headache, but to due to something else. She just wasn't sure what that something else was.

Looking back at her friend, Paris tried to make sense of it all. Charmaine was lying on top of the covers – white covers – that were now stained red with blood. *Charmaine's blood?*

Again, confusion filled Paris. *Why would there be blood in the bed? Hadn't the hotel washed the sheets properly?*

"Charmaine?" Tentatively Paris rolled her friend towards her and the moment she was facing Paris the horror of what she was looking at finally hit her, all confusion and sluggishness left her, Paris jumped out of bed and away from her friend as though she had been burned.

There Charmaine lay, lifeless, her eyes staring up at the ceiling, open, full of pain and horror. Paris closed her eyes and then opened them again, trying to remove the image she was seeing, but the horror was still there. Her best friend lay dead on the bed.

Feeling numb, Paris looked down and got a good look at her own body. For the first time, Paris realised she was covered in Charmaine's blood. There were also long, raw, bloody scratches on her arms and legs.

What the hell happened last night? Her mind screamed at her. How did one night of fun turn into a morning of horror, with no memory of what happened?

This could not be happening! The glint of a knife lying just above Charmaine's head caught Paris' attention and without thinking, she picked it up. Her mind tried to come to terms with what was happening, but it couldn't, it was too much, spots started swimming before her eyes, her head pounded and before the world went black, one terrifying thought ran through her head.

Did I kill my best friend last night?

When Paris came around, she was shocked to see that her nightmare was now her reality. Charmaine still lay dead on the bed beside her, while Paris still held the knife. Dropping it instantly as if it burned, she rose from the bed and started pacing the room. What was she going to do? She knew she should call the police, but if she did, her life would be over.

She would become what everyone at home had expected her to become. She would prove that, no matter how fast or how far you ran, your DNA always caught up with you.

Part of her didn't believe that she had done it, she was not a violent person. She was not like her parents. Paris valued life, and she loved her best friend more than anyone in this world.

Sitting on the floor, Paris rested her elbows on her knees and started rocking back and forth.

"What have I done? What have I done? What have I done?" She chanted over and over again.

She could feel her mind starting to snap, she needed to come up with a plan. She needed time to figure out what happened. She couldn't remember anything from last night and as it stood, she knew that she was going to go to jail.

She could not allow that to happen, as much as she loved her friend, she could not lose the freedom she had fought so hard to find, especially when she didn't even know if she had killed her or not.

Looking back at the bed, Paris looked for any change, but Charmaine still lay there, her dull eyes peering up at the ceiling. The stark white sheets stained with the bright red blood screamed at her, reminding her that her best friend was gone. As she stared, Paris realised the extent of what her friend had gone through, the slits cut into her dress from where the knife had been plunged into her friend's body repeatedly, and from the look of pain that was permanently etched on Charmaine's face, Paris truly believed that she had felt every stab of the knife.

Tears began to fall down Paris' face. There was no way she could have killed Charmaine like that, she was the one person who had loved Paris for herself. She never tried to change her, she only encouraged and supported Paris in everything she did. *NO*, she would not believe that she had done it. Paris needed time, and she knew that if she ended up in prison, that was something she would not have.

Rising from the floor, Paris strode into the bathroom, there on the mirror was a piece of paper, it was stuck there with a piece of gum.

On shaking legs, Paris reached forward to read it. She was

not going to touch it as she did not want her fingerprints on it. With bated breath, Paris began to read and with each word that greeted her, her blood turned to ice.

HELLO GIRL,

Congratulations on your graduation. I hope you like the present we got you. Try getting out of this one. Now we know you will do what you do best and run. But know that we will always find you.

HOW HAD THEY FOUND HER?

The shock Paris had been feeling earlier had worn off, now she was driven solely by fear.

Her best friend was gone, and now her father knew where she was, he was trying to drag her back into his world.

Paris sunk the floor placing her head in her hands. She didn't know what to do. Could she have done this? Did her father somehow force her into doing this and she just couldn't remember?

Everything she had been working for over the last four years was crashing down around her.

Paris looked around the room, there was no way she could go back to her old life now, but she would be damned if she would allow her father to drag her back into his world. She would do what she had done years ago; she would run.

Paris grabbed the shower cap and placed it over her hand like a glove, with fear and determination driving her forward, she re-entered the main room and rubbed off the fingerprints from the knife, and anything else she may have touched that would incriminate her in the murder of her friend.

She knew the police would eventually figure out she had been there, but for now she would try and give herself as much time as she could to get away. Paris didn't want to believe that she could have killed her friend, but she wasn't sure either way, but the one thing she did know was that if they police found, her fingerprints here and connected it to her past, they wouldn't even consider that she was innocent.

Paris washed any dishes she may have used and made the room look as though only one person had been there. Paris didn't believe that she had killed her best friend, and yet she couldn't take any chances.

Once that task had been completed, Paris made her way to the bathroom, stripped, washed herself and then packed up every last thing she had brought with her.

Walking over the bed, she bent down, kissed her best friend's cheek, and then walked to the door, shower cap back in place.

"I'm so sorry, Char. But I will figure out what happened to you." Paris promised before she walked out of the room, closing the door on her past forever.

Walking towards the back of the hotel, Paris took the stairs down to the lobby, where she walked out of the building as though everything was normal.

Catching the train, she made her way home, there she grabbed all of her belongings, and her car and made her way out of Seattle, away from a life that she could no longer have. She had no idea where she was going, or how she was going to live, but she knew she had about three months to figure it out.

In three months' time her study visa ran out, that was when she would be forced to go home. Before now she had never considered not living in America; once she graduated the plan was to get a full-time job, and eventually apply for citizenship. Now her life was a ticking time bomb. Three months was all she had before her past came knocking. She had to stay hidden, and she had to figure out a way to prove that she was innocent of Charmaine's murder, otherwise her family would win, one way or another.

CHAPTER THREE

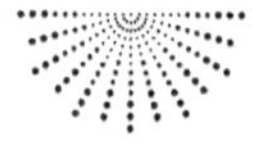

Paris had been driving for days.

It had been three days of little to no sleep, while living on nothing but junk food. She was not ready to slow down yet. Paris didn't feel like she was far enough away from the scene to relax even a little.

She had left Washington State and was now entering Montana. Paris knew she would have to get off the main highways and start taking the backroads soon.

When she had left Seattle, Paris had had a plan to try and trade her car for a different one, but the more she thought of it the more concerned she became.

She considered going to a dealer, then thought better of it, with a dealer came questions. And trying to sell or swap it privately was just too much hassle. She even considered dumping it and just buying an old banger, but she did not have the funds for that. She needed to save her money as it was all she had.

So that left her with hiding. Paris did however use some of the knowledge her father had endowed her with, late one night she had pulled into a quiet rest stop and while everyone was sleeping, she stealthily swapped her number plates with that of another car. She wasn't proud of it, but she knew it would buy her some more time.

She knew, however, that the less her car was seen, the better. She didn't know if anyone was looking for her yet, and she didn't want to find out. She hadn't listened to any news channels; she didn't want to know what was happening. Paris couldn't think when fear was taking control, and she knew the minute she listed to the news and heard about her friend, fear would follow.

Paris thought that they wouldn't be looking for her just yet. As far as they knew she hadn't been with her friend that night. They would come looking to speak with her, but she would not be their number one suspect, *yet*.

As far as anyone knew, she could simply be out for the day. It would be a few weeks before they started to get suspicious, and by then she would be in hiding. The good thing about America was that it was big and had lots of places to hide. She just had to find the right place.

For now though, she needed to start thinking about getting off of the main road and start taking some backroads. She would have less chance of being pulled over there.

As though the universe was listening to her, a sign came into view, indicating that the turnoff for Yellowstone National Park was two and half miles ahead.

That was perfect.

Paris took the turnoff and an hour and half later, she was entering Yellowstone. She drove through the park until she came to the main town near Old Faithful.

Paris considered driving on, but Yellowstone had been on her bucket list of places to see, and since she didn't know what her future held, Paris could not pass up this opportunity.

Parking the car, Paris got out and walked her way along

the wooden pathway, watching tourists as they took photos and enjoyed their lives. Paris reflected on how simple her life had been days ago. She had been as carefree and as happy as the tourists that now surrounded her.

A person who took happy snaps with the ones she loved.

A person who had laughed and enjoyed life.

How things changed in just a few short hours.

Now Paris wondered if she would ever laugh again.

Paris lowered her head, blocked out all of the happy sounds and continued on her walk. It didn't take long for her to reach the geyser, the sound of its ferocity drowned out the world around her, if only for a few minutes.

Walking up to the railing in front of her, Paris leaned over it and waited for the old geyser to unleash its power and energy. She didn't have to wait long before hot water spewed from the depths of the earth reaching up like it wanted to touch the sky. The sounds of awe and laughter were drowned out by the fury of the powerful display from Mother Nature.

As she watched, Paris contemplated her life as the geyser released its power time and again.

With each burst her own anger grew.

How had everything changed so drastically?

How had her family found her?

How was she going to prove she was innocent and save herself from being sent home?

All she had wanted to do was let her hair down, she deserved a little bit of that. It had taken a lot of hard work and courage to reach the point she was at last night, and with one mistake, one chance encounter, that freedom was going to be taken from her.

That freedom had also cost her the one person she could talk to, her rock, her saviour, her best friend.

A tear rolled down her cheek as the memory of Charmaine laying on the bed flashed through her mind.

"Are you alright, Love?" An old lady next to her asked.

Turning in surprise, Paris wiped the tear away before plastering a fake smile on her face.

"Yes, thank you. I am just amazed at how beautiful it is here." The lie came effortlessly, it was easy to be overcome by the beauty of this place.

"Oh, I agree. I have waited years to come here and witness this."

Paris nodded. She knew how the elderly woman felt.

Now that she had assured the elderly woman that she was fine, Paris hoped that she would once again be left to her own thoughts, but that was not to be.

"Would you mind taking a photo of myself and my husband, Dear?"

Paris wanted nothing more than to be left alone. She didn't want to talk to anyone, let alone interact with them. However, she had never been able to be rude to people. Especially elderly people. Growing up, Paris had always wished to have the kind of grandparents that all the kids around her seemed to have.

But, like most of her life, that was just one more wish that hadn't come true. Her grandparents had been just as corrupt as her father; it was the family business after all.

It was because of this that Paris valued every little kindness she could find or offer in the world. So, even though she wanted to be left alone to figure out her life, she turned to the elderly couple, smiled and replied, "not at all."

Paris took the camera that the lady was holding out.

Taking a step back, Paris waited for Old Faithful to show his fury once more, before taking the snap. "Thank you," the older man replied, taking back the camera.

"Are you staying around here?" he asked once they were back at the railing.

"No, just passing through," Paris answered, she hoped they didn't ask too many more questions, she would feel obliged to answer them out of politeness, and thanks to her father she had become a pro at making up lies on the spot. And considering that Paris wanted to stay under the radar as much as possible, answering personal questions would only hinder that task.

"Where are you headed to next?" The old woman asked, excitement lacing her voice.

Thankfully Paris would be able to answer that question without giving anything away because she really did not have any clue as to where she was going. "Not sure. I am on a bit of a road trip. I have no place set in my mind. I simply want to travel and find beauty in the world again." *And try and find my mind,* Paris added as an internal afterthought.

"Oh, a journey of self-discovery. I *love* it." The old man replied with a smile.

"Well if it is beauty you want to see, you should head to a small town just east of here called Cooke City. There is a little café there and they make the most amazing hot choco-lates and burgers." His wife added.

"Oh yes, it is a must." The old man chimed in for effect. Paris gave a short laugh, she was not sure that burgers and hot coffee fell into the category of finding beauty in the world, but with any luck it would keep her off the beaten track for a few more days. Giving the older couple a smile she offered. "With an endorsement like that, how can I refuse?"

The smiles the pair gave her were radiant, and if only for

a small moment, Paris was glad she could bring joy to someone's day.

But that feeling of happiness was ripped away from her the moment she saw two friends walking by enjoying each other's company the way her and Charmaine had.

The thought of Charmaine brought back the crippling feeling of loss, pain and fear. It became hard for her to breathe and Paris knew it was time to get going. She couldn't stay in one place for long, she had to keep moving. The urgency of her situation was brought back to her like a wave crashing against the shore. Taking a deep breath to settle her nerves, the brought forward her fake smile and offered the couple a farewell.

"Well I had better get going. Which way is Cooke City?" She asked.

"It's easy to find, simply head back to the main part of town, then turn left at the museum and follow that road. You can't get lost; there are signs the whole way there." The elderly man directed.

"Make sure you look out for all the animals along the way. They are simply magnificent."

Paris, thanked them and shook their hands but not before promising to take note of all the animals in the park. She also accepted a brochure from them that listed the said animals before taking her leave.

GETTING INTO THE CAR, Paris followed the instruction the

gentleman had given her and headed back towards the museum. As she passed the beautiful hotel that was situated in the main street, Paris considered staying in Yellowstone for a few nights, but after seeing how many people were here at this time of year, she thought better of it.

She needed to stay in a small, remote place. A place where no-one would question her about where she came from.

Once she was on the road she knew that she had made the right decision, she had wanted to stay off the main roads, and the direction she was driving now was exactly what she needed; it was secluded, it was picturesque, and it was quiet.

As she continued the drive, and the animals that were in the brochure kept appearing Paris hoped that she would find somewhere permanent to hide out for a while, and soon.

Somewhere where she could lose herself and wait until her memory came back. Paris just hoped that when it did, it didn't bring the horrifying truth that she *was* her parents' daughter; she could not handle knowing she was as evil as them.

"Dear Lord, please do not let it come about that I had any part in what happened."

It wasn't often that Paris prayed, she wasn't even sure she believed. But right now, she needed faith in something, and as her faith in herself was faltering she decided she would give anything a go.

CHAPTER FOUR

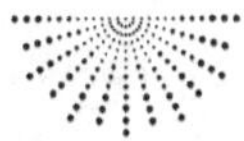

Pulling up in front of the restaurant the couple had directed her to, Paris turned off the car, but she didn't get out.

She couldn't just yet.

Instead Paris sat forward and just stared at the entrance, trying to decide if she would go in. Apart from the few hours at Yellowstone this would be the first real stop she had made in days. The most she had done was stop long enough for a quick nap, but she knew that, if she were to drive on much further, she would need to have some sort of a plan. She also was quite aware, now that burgers were just there, how hungry she was. The last decent meal she'd had, had been the last one she had shared with Charmaine; and that meal she didn't even remember.

Looking through the large glass windows, Paris could tell that there appeared to be no-one inside. She wasn't afraid of running into any police officers here, as the town was tiny, there didn't even appear to be any police office here. Her main worry was that there would be a TV. That would be the only way she would be found out.

She wasn't sure if the incident had made the news or not, but Paris didn't want to be anywhere near a T.V just in case.

Looking, she could see a T.V and she guessed that she couldn't hide from them forever.

Paris contemplated starting the car and just driving, but her stomach growled, putting a stop to all thoughts of leaving.

With her mind made up Paris decided to stop just long enough to make a plan and eat something. It would only be something small though.

Paris decided she would have a hot chocolate and order some fries. That wouldn't take too long.

Getting out of the car, she made her way inside. Her heart was racing, she was just waiting for someone to call her out, for someone to start pointing and calling her a murder, but when that didn't happen, she started to relax, a little.

The café was quaint and rustic.

Moose antlers adorned the wall, while knickknacks covered all possible spare surfaces. Turning around Paris continued to examine the room. It was like something straight out of a country movie.

The tables that were off to the right in the dining room were covered in black and white checked tablecloths with little wooden animals from the National Park as the centrepiece.

A smile played on Paris' lips as she enjoyed the homeliness of the café, and when she realised that the T.V. was not going to be turned on, the feeling of calm continued to overcome her.

Paris continued to roam the entrance of the café, enjoying the pictures on the wall of the area from decades ago, and it wasn't long before a petite older lady joined her.

"May I help you?" she asked startling Paris out of her perusal.

Paris turned to face the woman. She barely reached Paris' shoulders, and was what one would call portly. Her black hair, streaked with grey was pulled back with a clip, and the smile that she was bestowing on Paris reached her eyes, making them as warm as the interior of the café.

Paris decided that she would try something a little more than just chips.

"What do you recommend having with hot chocolate?"

Paris was pleased when the woman's smile widened.

"Oh, my famous apple pie and ice-cream go magnificently with hot chocolate."

Paris loved the way her accent sounded, as though she too was from the Wild West.

"Well then, I guess apple pie and ice-cream it is, as well as a hot chocolate."

"You won't be disappointed I promise. That will be three dollars and twenty-five cents."

Even though Paris had lived in the States for four years, she was till surprised sometimes with how cheap food was. Paris handed her a five-dollar note.

"Keep the change." She offered as way of a tip.

It was common practice in America to tip the waitress, however when it came to small diners like this one where the owner was the waitress, Paris was unsure of what to do, so tipped just to be sure.

She must have done the right thing, as the lady smiled kindly before saying, "Thank you Love, God bless you. Now go and have a seat, dear; your order won't be long."

"Thank you," Paris replied.

Turning she made her way into the dining room, once there she went straight to a table right by the window, not far from the door. It was the perfect place to position herself in case she had to make a quick getaway.

While she waited for her meal to arrive, she watched the

world pass by her. She was surprised to see deer wondering down the road as though it was an everyday occurrence. The people of the town didn't seem fazed. They simply went about their shopping, and banking. There was not much to the town, it was simply a small mountain town, with one main street.

There was a tavern, post office, a bank, a hairdresser, a local store, service station and the rest of the town was made up of hotels and cafes. Paris got the feeling that this town was more of a tourist destination. The tavern was situated across the road from where she sat, and Paris watched as people came and went, laughing and enjoying life. She wanted more than anything to go back to her life like that.

She loved joking and laughing with Charmaine... *had* loved.

Closing her eyes, Paris tried to recall what happened the night they had gone out. She went back to the last moment she remembered. But try as she might, the only thing she remembered was waking up.

The images of her friend lying dead had no trouble in rearing their ugly head. If only the rest of the night would be so accommodating Paris thought bitterly. She sighed, she was not going to give up.

Paris owed Charmaine the truth.

Pushing deeper into her mind, she tried once more to remember. She was just about to give up when images started to form through the fog.

Faintly Paris could picture two guys making their way over to their table. With that image more of the night became clearer.

Two guys *had* come over to their table. Paris had been dubious for some unknown reason, but Charmaine had reminded her that they were there to let their hair down.

It was because of that reminder that Paris pushed the

niggling feeling away and accepted the drink from the darker haired man, a man who looked vaguely familiar to her. She tried to place where she knew him from but couldn't pick it. She wondered if that was the reason behind her feeling of unease. Paris' head started to pound as she tried to remember more, she was not ready to give up, but no matter how hard she tried to push, all she could remember were their faces, not their names nor what happened next.

Opening her eyes, she grabbed a notebook and pen out of her bag and listed as many details as she could about the men who had offered them drinks. She made a circle around the dark-haired man's description and added a question mark. Even if she couldn't remember the names, at least if it came down to her being arrested, she could still give a description of the men to the police. She wasn't sure at this point if they had anything to do with what happened later that night, but her gut was telling her they were right smack in the middle of it.

Closing her eyes once more, Paris pushed harder, she tried to focus on what they were saying. She needed something, anything that would give her a clue as to what happened next.

But nothing came.

The small headache that had started to play at the back of her mind, was becoming more forceful. She knew she had to stop before she gave herself a migraine.

Anger boiled up inside of her as the headache started to push the memories away. The only thing that was clear to her was the sight of her friend lying dead on the bed.

Why couldn't she remember?

Paris wanted to scream and curse the world for what was happening to her, but instead she had to pretend to the world that everything was okay, while inside she was shattering.

Paris was pulled from the hunt through her memories by the owner's voice.

"Here you go, Love. Enjoy."

Opening her eyes, Paris gave her a smile before thanking her.

"Is everything okay?" The woman asked, a small frown marring her face.

"Yes, thank you." Paris replied.

She hoped she hadn't said anything while she had been trying to find the answer she sought.

"Alright, but if you need anything else just holler." She offered.

"I will thank you. You were right, this looks absolutely delicious." Paris extended warmly.

The smile thankfully returned to the owner's face. She gave Paris a nod of approval before returning to the counter. Even though the woman was busy doing other things, Paris felt as though she was still watching her, so she dug into her food and pretended to watch the world around her as though she had not a care in the world.

Thankfully the owner's attention was drawn to the door when a woman with two children entered the café.

"Hey Kris." The customer greeted as she tried to rein in the children.

"Hey Carly, how are the munchkins today?"

Paris watched the two children jump from foot to foot trying to tell the owner, Kris, all about their exciting news.

It warmed Paris to see that in all the darkness that surrounded her there was still light in the world. She knew she shouldn't be watching the exchange, but she just couldn't take her eyes from the children.

Had she ever been that happy as a child?

"Hold up, I can't understand you both at the same time."

Kris laughed walking around the counter, where she leant down on her knees.

The oldest one, who looked about eight, threw herself into Kris' arms before pulling back and finishing her story. "We are going on a trip. Mom even pulled us out of school."

"Is that right. And just where are you going on this special trip?" Kris asked them.

"Black-something Ranch." The boy, who couldn't have been any older than six, answered.

Paris watched as their mother shook her head at their excitement. Kris stood and smiled at her. It was obvious to Paris that the woman was quite close with this family.

"Why are you going down there this time?" She asked a smile playing on her face.

"Oh, don't get me started." Carly laughed.

Paris found the conversation intriguing. The way in which the Carly answered Kris told Paris that she was exasperated about the task, and at the same time a little excited.

"How long will you be gone?" Kris asked as she walked them into the dining area.

Paris continued to eat her lunch and tried to appear as though she was not listening to everything that was said. She knew it was rude to eavesdrop, but she couldn't help it. Paris needed to be drawn into something, anything that would allow her to forget about her troubles, even if only for a short time.

"Probably about two months, I would like to make it a month, but I won't know until I get there."

"Right, so when do you leave?"

Carly looked at her children before giving Kris a long painful look.

"As soon as we are done here." She answered with a sigh.

Kris laughed, "I see, so do you want the usual today?" Kris asked.

"Yes please, and can you do some to go as well, it is going to be a long drive to Cody."

"Sure thing, Sweets. Won't be long." And with that Kris left the dining area to go and get Carly's order ready.

"When can we go?" The boy whined.

"When we have had some lunch and after we pack the car." Carly replied with patience.

"Excuse me, you dropped this." Paris heard a soft, sweet little voice announce.

Looking to her side, she saw the little girl holding out her phone. Paris noticed how much like her mother the young girl looked. She had brown hair that was drawn up into a pigtail with a pink ribbon tied into it.

Her brown eyes shone with merriment and Paris wanted nothing more than to have the worries of this young lady.

"Miss?" The young girl prompted when Paris said nothing. That was when Paris remembered that she was holding her phone. Paris hadn't even realised it had fallen out of her pocket.

"Thank you." Paris replied, taking the phone from her tiny hands before putting it back in her coat. She wasn't afraid of anyone calling her as it wasn't turned on.

She hadn't wanted to answer anyone's calls. She knew that the police would question her as to why her phone had not been switched on, 'an innocent woman would not need to turn her phone off and hide,' she could hear the media and police say already.

But Paris had that all figured out, she would claim that she had been out of range and that was why she had not gotten anyone's messages.

The little girl nodded, then smiled before she returned to her seat, her mother smiled at Paris before asking, "Not from around here, are you?"

Paris considered giving the same short answers she normally gave when people asked her questions.

But for some reason, this woman made her ache for the friendship she was now missing, so Paris smiled and answered. "That obvious?"

Carly laughed. "Not at all, but I have lived here for nearly ten years now, so you get to know the locals. Where you headed?" It was a question that was becoming common for people to ask, and yet each time it was, Paris' heart sped up.

She couldn't help it.

She had a feeling that it would be this question that finally got her caught.

"Nowhere in particular, just travelling until I find the right place to stop."

Paris wondered if that answer would raise any suspicions, because in reality how many people who were on the up and up didn't know where they were going? Paris breathed a sigh of relief when she simply smiled and replied, "That sounds wonderful."

Paris noticed that Carly looked as though she was just about to say something else, but Kris returned with milkshakes and burgers galore, and any conversation they were about to have had been forgotten.

The children's faces lit up like it was Christmas, and as soon as they had said thank you, they were digging in. Carly was kept busy, trying to make sure that more food ended up in their mouths than on their clothes.

Paris decided that she was better off not conversing anymore, so ignoring the family she went back to eating her own meal so she could leave.

CHAPTER FIVE

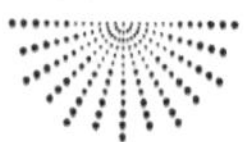

Carly shook her head as Kris laughed at her children as they dug into their meals as though they had never been taught any manners.

"So, what are you going to do with these two when you are there?"

Carly sighed. "I have no idea. I put an ad in the paper looking for a nanny for them, but everyone that applied was either too young or too inexperienced." Carly looked at her children and thought about the numerous woman who had applied. Her children would have eaten them alive.

"I need someone who can not only look after them, but also teach them something, or at least try and give them some short of education."

Kris laughed. "Don't worry, Sweets, you will find someone."

"I hope you are right, because if it doesn't happen soon, they will be getting their education from the ranch hands; and you *know* how that will go."

This time the laughter that came from Kris was big and booming. It filled the café and made the kids laugh as well.

Carly was enjoying her talk with Kris, this woman could always make her see the funny side of things. And the children absolutely loved her burgers. They were so good that they had become one of Carly's bribing tools.

"I know you said not to ask, but *why* are you heading down there this time." Carly was just getting ready to answer Kris when the phone rang.

"Darn, I will be right back Sweetie." Kris offered. Carly smiled at the frustration she could hear in the woman's voice. Carly knew there was nothing more Kris loved than a bit of gossip and boy was she going to love the latest she had on her brother.

"Take your time." Carly offered. She couldn't see her kids finishing anytime soon. Carly watched Kris rush away to answer the phone. She laughed when she saw her face light up upon answering it and the moment she sat down at the chair behind the counter Carly knew the woman was going to be there for a while. Smiling she turned to her own meal and tucked in with gusto.

Carly knew it would be a while before she had the chance to have burgers as good as these ones.

Damn Chance had better make this up to her.

This was it, this was the chance Paris had been waiting for. Here was a job that allowed her to still teach children yet hide at the same time.

In addition, Paris would probably be able to get Carly to pay her cash in hand, that way she wouldn't have to worry about tax or anything, and if she agreed, it would allow Paris to stay off the grid for a little longer.

Paris wanted nothing more than to yell at this woman to hire her, but she knew that if she did it, only make her come across as crazy. As she listened to the children laughing and joking, Paris sat there trying to formulate a plan.

Then Carly's phone rang, and it was then that Paris was given the exact cover story she needed.

"He wants *what?*" Carly had moved away from her children when she took the call and was standing just behind Paris' table. So even though she was talking low, Paris was able to hear everything.

"He already got the house in Seattle, he cannot have the car as well. *He* was the one that left *me* for a young piece of ass. *Fine,* you tell him that I will fight him. This conversation is over." And with that she hung up.

Paris turned in her chair to see a defeated Carly lean her head against her arm propped on the window.

"Is everything okay?" Paris asked.

When Carly looked at her, Paris lifted her hands in the air, "I wasn't eavesdropping I promise, I couldn't help but overhear."

Carly gave her a slight smile. "Never get married." She said on a small, bitter laugh.

"Guess I should thank my lucky stars that I got out early then. I mean he turned out to be crazy after just six months, I can't imagine what he would have been like after marriage."

Carly looked over at her children who were happily colouring in, and eating, before she took a seat across from Paris.

Paris secretly congratulated herself on getting this far, now all she needed to do was close the deal. She was still concerned that the woman sitting across from her could still leave. But the next question put Paris' fear to rest for the time being.

"What happened with yours?" Carly asked.

Paris knew that she should at least stay as close to the truth as possible *If you are going to tell a lie, keep it as close to the truth as possible."* Her mother used to always tell her. Paris laughed inside. She never thought her mother's twisted advice would ever come in handy.

"Not the same as you, in fact I only wish it were as simple as cheating on me. No offense." Paris could have kicked herself for being so stupid. She wanted Carly to feel sorry for her, but she had to be careful not to alienate her.

Carly smiled and waved her hand, before saying, "None taken. So, tell me what brings you to my neck of the woods?"

It was time for Paris to shine.

"Unfortunately, the home I grew up in was not a nice place. Fortunately, I was able to escape from there. But what I didn't know was that no matter how far I ran they were always looking for me. I had hoped that they would just forget about me and move on, but I was not so lucky." Paris cringed as she let a little of her true story out. Paris worried if she was doing the right thing, but when Carly leaned forward interested, Paris knew she had no option but to continue. She need money and this could be the perfect solution to her problems.

Paris was still trying to decide if she was going to continue, but Carly's next question decided that for her.

"Did they find you?"

Paris nodded solemnly.

"What happened, if you don't mind me asking?" Carly added, her eyes were filled with curiosity. Paris looked over at the children who were happily unaware of the tension that was running through her. Paris would have given anything to have had a childhood like the one they obviously have.

"Well I had been seeing this guy for six months; stupidly I was convinced he was falling in love with me. One night I came home from work and I heard him on the phone. He was arguing with someone about how it wasn't the right time yet."

"He was working for your family, wasn't he?" Carly interrupted.

Paris gave a short laugh, one that did not contain any humour. "Yes, he was one of their cronies who had been sent to keep an eye on me. It was only after I threatened to leave and call the cops that he let me know the truth. They had hired him to bring me home, however he deemed necessary. He admitted that there was no real love between us, and that was not the worst of it. It turned out he was married with a real family back home and he was glad the truth was out so he could get home to them."

Paris felt a little bad at the sympathy she saw in Carly's eyes, while the part about him being a crony for her family was true, Paris added the bit about having a family because the truth would raise more questions than she was prepared to answer. The truth was he was her father's personal hitman. He was the man her father called into clean up his messes. That was exactly what her father considered her, a mess. But she could not explain all of that without explaining that her family was nothing but a bunch of career criminals.

"So did you call the police? I would have." Carly asked.

Paris shook her head. "There was nothing they could do, all he did was make me fall in love with him after all. So I left. I knew I couldn't stick around. But that didn't solve my problem. I knew that my family was never going to let me go that easily, and what made his betrayal even worse is that he has been texting and trying to find me ever since. Because he now sees me as a job he needs to finish. He has become my own personal stalker."

Paris looked down at the table; she didn't want Carly to see the lie in her eyes. The last part had only just come to her, she knew it would give her the perfect cover for asking for cash in hand as well as a reason why she never answered her phone.

Paris couldn't handle the silence that had fallen on the table. She worried that she might have laid it on to thick. Raising her eyes from the table she faced Carly who was looking at the table lost in her own thoughts.

Paris was just getting ready to say something when Carly beat her too it. Looking up from the table Carly's eyes met hers head on, "Well. Yes. Your situation is a little more complicated than mine. Thankfully, mine was just a philandering husband who couldn't keep it in his pants long enough to be a real family." Carly looked over at her children with love in her eyes. "I have to say though, I have two things that I *am* thankful to him for."

Paris smiled at the children and knew that this was her chance. It was now or never. She had just garnered her sympathy now it was time to garner Carly's help.

"Speaking of the children, I couldn't help but overhear before that you are in need of a nanny."

Carly turned back to Paris and smiled. "Offering, are you?"

Paris nodded. She laughed at the look of shock that crossed Carly's face. Of all the things that Paris could have agreed to, she didn't think Carly even considered that one of them.

"Don't seem so shocked. I need money, and it's a great way for me to stay off the grid."

At Carly's frown, Paris worried that she had gone too far. She probably shouldn't have used the words 'off the grid', normally only criminals used phrases such as that. She was showing too much of her upbringing and the last thing Paris needed was for Carly to do a background check on her. Paris' heart sped up when the image of the police showing up and arresting her entered her mind. The last thing Paris wanted, or needed, was for someone to look into her background. She needed to come with a plan and fast.

"I will do you a deal. I will come and be your nanny, but I will do it on a trial basis. If you don't like my work in the first few weeks, we can call it quits and you won't have to pay me anything. If you do deem me acceptable then you can pay me whatever rate you deem plausible, and I promise to give your kids a great education, one that doesn't involve horses, cattle or women of any kind."

Carly laughed at that.

"Do you have any prior qualification?"

"Considering that I was a primary school teacher before all of this, I would say yes."

Carly's eyes widened. Paris watched hopefully as she mulled over her options. She looked back at her kids who were laughing with Kris and then she stuck out her hand to shake Paris'.

"Guess today is my lucky day, Miss…?"

Paris quickly searched her mind for a name to use, when her grandmother's maiden name popped up, "Tailor," she offered. "Paris Tailor."

"Well Paris. I just have one more concern."

Paris held her breath she knew what was coming. She just hoped Carly accepted her answer and left it there.

"How far off the grid are we talking?"

Looking down Paris began to wring her hand together. This next part could blow all chances she had of getting this job.

"Like being paid cash in hand off the grid."

Paris watched as Carly's eyes narrowed.

"Why do you want to be paid cash in hand?"

Paris took a deep breath and prepared to tell her final lie, well she hoped it was the final one.

"Because, while my ex is looking for me, I would prefer to

make life as simple as possible. The less ways he has to track me the better. I just need a fresh start."

Paris held her breath as she watched Carly mull over the decision. She seemed to be taking her time, which made Paris a little nervous.

Paris had a feeling that she was going to say no, that was until her children started bickering. They were fighting over the same crayon. Carly took a deep breath and stood from the table, preparing to go and settle her children, but before she left, she looked at Paris once more before offering her hand to shake once more.

"I hope you are ready for an adventure." She added.

A huge smile spread across Paris' face. She couldn't believe it had worked. She was so thankful in that moment that she could have kissed this woman. Instead, she took her hand and shook it with vigour.

"I'm sure I will be fine. I am used to dealing with children." Paris couldn't understand why Carly found that funny.

"Well I have to go, but if you are serious about being their nanny, I will meet you here in two days' time. If you don't show up, I will understand, but I sincerely hope you do."

Paris took the card that Carly held out. Scrawled across the front was the name *Blackridge Ranch*, with the address below.

Yes, this was it, this was just the place she needed.

A ranch in the middle of nowhere in Wyoming was the perfect place to stay hidden.

"You can count on me being there." Paris replied as Carly rounded up her kids and headed for the door.

"I look forward to it." She said before she headed out. Paris took one more look at the card, before she placed it in her pocket. Standing, she thanked Kris for the lovely meal and opened the door to leave.

Walking outside, Paris took a deep breath of air; this was exactly what she needed.

Paris knew she would have to stop for the night; she also needed to figure out what she needed to get for her stay at the ranch, as well as plan the best route to take.

She was hoping that the place she picked to stay for the night had maps of the area, otherwise she would have to buy one, she was not willing to turn her phone on just yet, not even for navigation.

Paris smiled as she drove, everything would finally work itself out.

She had a way to get an income, and hopefully she would have the time she needed to figure out what happened to her friend. She knew her father was behind this, but she just had to figure out how.

As she drove on, the anger of losing her friend overtook the happiness she had just felt.

"I am going to get you for this you bastard." Paris hissed under her breath. Her father had gone too far this time. She promised herself that if it did turn out to be the work of her father, she was not going to just run this time.

This time she was going to take him down.

It was time she broke free from them forever.

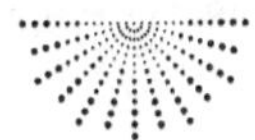

It had taken Paris exactly two days to drive down through Yellowstone National Park, along Bear Tooth highway, to Cody. Now she was driving just outside of Cody where the ranch was meant to be.

Unlike the mountains of Montana, the plains of Wyoming were vast and open, with rolling hills. The land stretched for miles and were only broken by the Rocky Mountains which ran the through the guts of America.

Still, the lush green grass that spread for miles, dappled with rolling hills and trees, was magnificent.

The sunsets here would be amazing.

Paris started to worry that she had gotten the address wrong. There was nothing out here. Surely a ranch would stand out against the backdrop of the rolling plains she thought to herself.

"Come on, where are you?" Paris growled leaning forward over her steering wheel. As she drove further down the road, with no ranch appearing, she considered turning around and heading back to Cody. Maybe there she could find a service station that could give her better directions.

"Just five more miles." She added.

Paris had almost reached the five-mile mark, when she saw it, she had never been so happy to see a place in her life.

On the right side of the road was a big steel arch with *Blackridge* written through it.

Paris indicated that she was turning, and the moment she drove under the arch, she had a feeling that her life was about to change, *again.*

The road she was driving down was dirt and felt as long as the five miles she had just driven, she tried to focus on the road, but the land around her kept on catching her eyes. Cattle dotted the landscape all around her, and she could see men on horses roving between them, to a backdrop of green mountains.

It was unbelievable. It was like something out of a western movie.

Ten minutes later, Paris was pulling up in front of a huge ranch house. And once again her breath was taken away.

It was as though someone had picked the house in front of her straight out of an old western movie and dropped it right in the centre of the ranch. The three stories of white timber and its wrap-around veranda had Paris feeling like she had stepped back in time.

She half expected a bunch of cowboys or Indians to greet her.

Shaking her head at her daydreaming, Paris parked the car and looked out over the rolling hills and plains beyond.

This place was glorious.

Off to the right about six hundred yards away were the stables and barn, and on the other side of the house, not far from it, must be the sleeping quarters for the farmhands. Paris only knew this because there were a few of them mulling around getting ready for the day. She had made sure to get here early, she didn't want Carly thinking that she had changed her mind.

Leaning against the car Paris took a deep breath, stretched her neck, then her arms above her head and exited the car. As her foot hit the ground, she admired the way the sun highlighted the clouds above the house with hues of orange as it rose for the morning. The sight was spectacular.

Locking the door, she waited for a minute gathering her composure. Paris had no idea what to expect, she remembered Carly mentioning that this was her brother's ranch. She wondered how he would feel having a stranger staying here. She guessed there was only one way to find out. Paris took a deep breath and headed towards the house.

Her confidence faltered though the closer to the house she got, she was still about one yard from the door and she could hear yelling.

"Come on, Carls, you can't be serious!"

"Oh, darn right I am serious, Chance!"

"Two months. Why two months?"

"Because after going through all of the paperwork that has been sent over, I have worked out it will take me *that* long to sort this mess out."

"You are over exaggerating *again*. *If* you let me handle it my way, I would have it sorted out in less than a week."

"If I let you handle it your way, I will be bailing your ass out of jail *again*."

The closer Paris got to the door, the louder the yelling seemed to get. Paris wondered if she should knock on the door, but she didn't want to get in the middle of whatever was going on in there.

She was just getting up the nerve to knock on the door when the husky voice once again broke through the tension-filled silence.

"Damn! Fine! You can stay here for two months, but as I told you the other day when you arrived, don't be thinking you can order me around. Even though this is *our* ranch, *I* run it. Besides, I am a grown-ass man, I do *not* need my big sister telling me what to do."

"Well, if you had listened to your big sister in the first place, we wouldn't be in this mess to start with." Carly bit back. Paris waited to see if any more yelling would be forth coming, but the only sounds that greeted her was the scraping of a chair against the wooden floor, followed by footsteps. It appeared as though the fight was over, yet Paris still hesitated.

"It's good to have you home." The male voice offered at a lower tone than before.

"It's good to be home." Carly replied.

"Well I guess I had better get some work done, the boys are probably already out in the field waiting for me, I will probably see you at dinner. If I am not back, eat without me as usual."

Paris waited for Carly's brother to come out the front door, but after a few minutes had passed and nobody emerged, she assumed that Chance had either gone out another way or had was somewhere else in the house. Now was as good a time as any to make herself known.

Knocking on the door, Paris held her breath and waited for it to be answered.

"When did you become such a chicken?" she berated herself as her heart pounded.

Paris listened as footsteps drew closer to the door. Paris was relieved to see the smile that crossed Carly's face as she opened the door.

"Thank God you came. I have been out of my mind trying to keep the rugrats occupied while working. Come in. Come in. I can't believe you are here so early."

Paris' heart rate started to come back down to a normal pace at Carly's greeting. She was half expecting her to have changed her mind.

"I didn't want you to change your mind," Paris joked.

Carly laughed. "I was more worried that you would have changed yours."

Carly moved aside and let Paris enter the house. Paris looked around taking in her surroundings. If she thought the outside of the house of magnificent, it was nothing compared to the inside.

Everywhere she looked she could see wood. The roof, the floor and the stairs that lead up to the second floor were all made of polished wood. She had no idea what type it was, but it was beautiful.

And much like the outside, the inside looked like something from an old western movie. The walls had a few cattle horns placed strategically, while other parts of the wall housed guns of all types.

Paris still could not get over how lax the American's were about showcasing guns for everyone to see. The rest of the walls were covered in family photos.

Paris' inspection of the room was brought to a halt when Carly yelled out, "Leo. Nerada. Come here please."

"Yes Mom." They yelled in unison, before the pitter-patter of their feet could be heard coming from upstairs.

"I hope you don't mind starting right away. I will take you on a tour of the house with the children, so you know where everything is, but then I would love it if I could try and get some work done. I have some important business I have been trying to take care of and it would be a great help if you could amuse these two." She continued as the children joined them.

Paris smiled at the two adorable children in front of her. She had forgotten how cute they were. They were staring at her with beaming smiles. Paris didn't know if she should be flattered or worried.

She decided that she would start of on the right foot. Putting on her best teacher voice, Paris looked directly at them before replying.

"That is no trouble at all. I would love to spend some time getting to know them."

"Great. We will sort the rest of the details out over dinner tonight."

"Perfect." Paris smiled.

"Children, this is Paris and she is going to be your new nanny."

"Aren't you the lady from the café the other day?" Nerada asked, a smile on her face.

Yep, these two were sharp as tacks, Paris thought. Not all six and eight-year olds were that observant. Most of them forgot about what they ate for lunch, let alone who they had met days ago.

"I sure am. Thank you once again for returning my phone."

"You are very welcome. I like her, Mom." Nerada informed Carly.

"Good. Then let's try not to scare this one off shall we." Paris looked at the children and their wide smiles. They looked like butter wouldn't melt in their mouths, but Carly's last comment had Paris realising that they probably had a wild streak in them.

Paris knew she would have to keep on her toes around these two.

She was pleased though when both Nerada and Leo nodded their heads in agreement.

"Right, let's get this show on the road." Carly instructed as they started making their way through the ranch house.

With each new room they entered, coupled with children's chatter and Carly's explanation, Paris started to relax. This was just what she needed.

This was where she was going to figure out what had happened in Seattle, because Paris could finally say without doubt that no matter what truth came out she was not responsible in any way for her best friend's death, she knew deep down inside, no matter the circumstances, she was not a killer.

Just knowing that she was taking some of the pressure off of Carly after what her dick of an ex was doing to her reminded Paris how much she hated anyone suffering, she felt for the young woman in front of her. There was no way she could have hurt someone she loved so brutally.

It was going on midnight. Looking over at the clock sitting on her bedside table, Paris sighed. She knew she needed sleep, but as it was every night for the past week, the moment she closed her eyes, images of Charmaine's mutilated body rushed forward.

Paris was beyond feeling grief for her friend, now she was just angry. She had spent the first few nights on the run feeling sorrow and pain for what her friend had endured, but on the third day when the reality of what had happened and the possibility of why it had happened settled into her bones, the anger set it.

It was like an anger she had never felt before. Her body hummed with it. She wanted nothing more than to extract revenge on those who had done this; and one way or another she would.

Paris still didn't know where the police were at with the

investigation, she was still too afraid to find out if they had figured out that she had been there, or even if she had been named as a suspect. Once that happened Paris knew it would be next to impossible for her to stay off the radar. She knew it was isolated out here, but it was not so isolated that they did not get news. And the murder of a young teacher at a hotel in Seattle would be headline news. Even in remote Wyoming.

With that thought now at the forefront of her mind, Paris knew that sleep would be useless tonight.

Getting out of bed, Paris made her way over to the window seat that lay beneath the bay window in her room. Paris had fallen instantly in love the moment Carly had shown her this room. It was at the rear of the ranch house and faced the mountains that was the backdrop to the ranch.

The bed was huge and was covered in a white comforter that felt like it was filled with feathers and was as soft as it looked. But the window seat and fireplace that covered one wall made it Paris' dream room.

It was strange being in a new house, she was not used to the noises that she could hear all around her. The wooden floors under her feet creaked as she walked, and she could swear she could hear the howl of a wolf off in the distance.

The shadows of the cupboard that sat across from the bed left a pattern on the floor as the moonlight shone into the room.

Paris should have felt uncomfortable in her new surroundings, but somehow the peace and safety that this house offered worked to soothe her jittery nerves.

Sitting down Paris pulled the throw rug that was sitting on the end of the bench across her legs and stared out over the night sky.

It was beautiful here, if she had thought the ranch was

spectacular during the day, it was nothing compared to what she was seeing now.

The dark night sky stretched for miles over open fields, and the stars that lit it up took her breath away. She had never seen the sky look so clear, or never had she seen so many stars. All of her life, Paris had grown up in cities, where the pollution of the lights drowned out the magnificence of the stars.

Now sitting here, she was sorry that she hadn't gotten the chance to see this before.

Paris' only wish was that she could have been here for any other reason. Thinking back over the day a smile spread across her face. Leo and Nerada were two little bundles of mischief, mayhem and wonder. And she had loved every minute she had spent with them.

Being with them made her miss teaching. It brought back all the reasons why she had gotten into the profession in the first place.

She couldn't wait to start teaching them tomorrow.

She had not been able to do any teaching today, but tomorrow would be a different story. Paris had already made plans on what she was going to do.

Today had simply been spent getting to know them, and she had learnt a lot.

She had learnt that their Uncle Chance along with their mother owned the farm.

Carly had lived here before she had been married, but a year after her wedding, her husband had gotten work at Yellowstone and so they had made the move to Cooke Town, where they still resided. Paris couldn't help but laugh when Leo had informed her that they were back down here because Uncle Chance had 'become friends' with the wrong lady again. His mother's words apparently, he even did the air quotes.

Paris was sure that the uncle in question would not be happy having his business spoken about in front of strangers, so she had simply nodded and changed the subject.

Paris still hadn't met the mysterious Chance, not that she really wanted or needed to. He had left before she had entered the house and as he had predicted, he hadn't shown up for dinner.

As Paris sat staring out of the window, she tried to picture what he would look like. She tried to imagine him based on voice. She wondered if he would be as gruff looking as his voice sounded, or would he be one of the types of people that looked nothing like what you pictured.

Paris decided that he probably looked a bit like Carly, only manlier, she smiled to herself and looked towards the bunkhouse, wondering if he was in there somewhere.

She was not sure why she was so fixated on figuring this out, she was just happy that it was currently taking her mind of other things.

As Paris continued to stare out the window it was as though her thoughts conjured him up, she watched as a figure sauntered over from the barn towards the house.

Paris understood that in reality, this man could be any number of persons who lived on the farm, but deep down she knew it was him.

She knew it by the authority that he held as he walked; an authority one gained from being the owner of a ranch.

As the moon shone, lighting up the night, she could see he was wearing the typical cowboy get-up consisting of denim jeans, black t-shirt with a plaid shirt thrown over, and cowboy boots to complete the look; the only thing that was missing was the hat that he was carrying in his hands.

Paris was a little disappointed that she couldn't make out much more from this distance.

What she could see though, was a man who was all muscle.

It rippled with every step he took.

It wasn't the sculpted type of muscle that men got from spending days in a gym, no, it was the kind a man got from hard work; days of working under the sun, lifting heavy things.

The other thing that caught Paris' attention was that he was tall. Well over six feet. Paris was a sucker for tall men.

Paris continued to watch him from the safety of her dark room.

She knew she should not be spying on him, it was almost perverted the way she watched him, but Paris couldn't help it. She couldn't take her eyes from him.

The butterflies in her stomach were new for her.

It was unusual that any man had this effect on her. Especially since the debacle of her last relationship. Paris knew that looks did not make the man, sometimes it actually meant nothing but trouble.

Since then Paris had become adept at keeping control of her feelings. Feelings, when it came to men, only caused her pain.

But for some unknown reason Paris was having difficulty relaying that message to her brain right now. Her body and her mind were betraying her. She was acting as though she was some horny teenager.

Paris knew she had to stop watching him, but as she gazed at him, he stopped, just before he reached the stairs, and looked straight up into her room, and she couldn't look away if she wanted to.

Her breath caught in her throat, as she waited for something to happen.

She knew he couldn't see her, but it felt as though he was

searching for her. The fantasy was broken when he disappeared onto the porch. She listened as he opened the door
and continue into the house.

Paris continued to hold her breath as she listened to him
walk through the house, up the stairs and along the hallway.
Then the steps stopped right outside of her room, and for a
moment she thought he was going to enter her room.

But the door across the hall opening and closing let her
know that she was safe tonight. Paris she took her first deep
breath since seeing him.

Shaking her head at her own stupidity, Paris quietly made
her way back to bed, where she climbed in and buried herself
deep below the feathered quilt.

What was wrong with her?

The last thing she needed at the moment was to lose her
mind over a guy. She was not going to be able to enjoy a
normal life until the mess of her present was cleaned up.
Finding out what had happened to her friend and getting her
justice was the only thing that mattered.

Paris' heart hurt as thoughts of the fun times her and
Charmaine used to have washed over her. If Charmaine had
been here, the two of them would have discussed at lengths
the attributes of the ranch owner. They would have swooned
over him together. Charmaine would have been the one to
encourage Paris to take a chance on him,

But the days of ogling men, drinking lemonade on their
porch or watching horror movies until they were too scared
to go to bed, were gone forever, and the knowledge of that
filled her with a gaping hole of loss.

Paris wondered how her life would ever be the same
again. She just wished she knew could remember what
happened so that she could give not only Charmaine, but
also her family, some closure and justice but so that she
could also get rid of her past once and for all.

Closing her eyes, Paris feel into a restless sleep, one filled with the continuous nightmares that mashed reality with monsters.

CHAPTER SEVEN

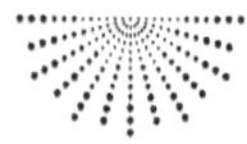

Chance stepped out of the shower, wrapped a towel around himself and walked to the vanity. Rubbing the fog off the mirror he studied himself, deciding if he needed a shave or not.

Normally he would not worry about little things such as shaving, but with his sister here, he knew he had to make a bit more of an effort to look presentable, he didn't need her on his back about anything else. Even though he was a grown man, his sister still liked to mother him.

Taking one more look, Chance decided on not, a few more days would not make a difference. He was just about to dry himself when his phone tinged on the basin.

Picking it up, he groaned when he saw who it was from.

Come on baby, talk to me. I am sorry about all the mess our misunderstanding has caused, but if you had just kept your promise then none of this would be happening. I can make all of this go away if you would just talk to me.

Chance snorted, hit the back key and placed his phone back on the basin. There was no way in hell he was going to talk to *her*; not only had his lawyers advised against anymore contact between them, he was also not *that* stupid.

He was done with the woman.

In fact, he was done with all women.

This was the last time he was going to allow a woman to try and ruin his life. For Christ's sake he had only slept with her few times, but Liz had gotten it in her head that they were in a long-term relationship.

Why did women have to be like that?

Chance knew he was in trouble the minute she had started talking about moving in. At first Chance had tried to be subtle in his rejection, and instead of telling her flat out that he wanted to end it, he had started by seeing less of her, cancelling plans that kind of thing, hoping that she would get the message and slow things down.

But the day she had started placing her belongings in his bathroom and bedroom, he knew it was time to call it quits and that was when he had pulled the brakes on the whole thing.

That night Change sat Liz down at dinner and explained that he wasn't after anything serious and suggested that it was time they went their own way.

Chance had thought that all things considered he had handled the situation well, the only problem was Liz didn't see the situation the way he did.

Once he had explained to her what he was thinking, she had become quite aggressive, yelling at him, she even threw some of his dishware at him. Apparently, Liz had gotten it into her head that they were the real deal; that he was eventually going to marry her.

Chance was exasperated with the whole situation, and when Liz had picked up another cup to hurl at him, Chance grabbed her by the arm and escorted her out of the house.

"You will be sorry for this." She had screamed at him. Chance simply closed the door and headed to the kitchen to clean up the mess.

Liz did not leave straight way, she proceeded to pound on the door. "Chance, open this door right now." She had screamed at the top of her lungs.

When Chance didn't, she tried another tactic. Her voice had turned seductive, as she tried to seduce him with all types of pleasure. But Chance was not interested in what that pleasure came with.

Finally, Liz gave up, Chance listened as she stomped off the veranda and headed to her car, swearing and cursing him the whole way.

As Chance cleaned up the mess, he signed to himself. The sad part about the whole situation was that this wasn't the first time this scenario had happened to him. Chance had just been lucky that the previous experiences hadn't threatened his livelihood.

He wasn't naive, Chance knew that it wasn't him the women wanted, he was good in bed, but he wasn't *that* good.

No, what they wanted was his money.

They wanted to marry him so they could spend their lives in luxury, spending his money while he worked hard.

But what they didn't understand when they started dating him, was there was never any chance of them getting it.

His parents had built this ranch from nothing, and the only way anybody, other than Carly, would get their hands on it or the money they made was over his dead body.

He was not going to marry a woman until he knew for sure that it was him they wanted.

That feat, however, was turning out to be harder than he first thought.

As his friend, Bronx, often said, *bitches be crazy*.

Chance thought back on the last year and his dating

issues and it seemed that the crazy ones seemed to be coming out of the woodwork.

Chance looked at himself once more, then huffed.

He knew he would have to deal with Liz sooner or later, but right now; he preferred later.

For now, he would leave it in Carly's capable hands.

This was not the first time his sister had come down here to help him out of a tight situation. While he loved having his sister and his niece and nephew here, he hated that he had stuffed up once more.

He may be younger, but Chance was supposed to look after her, not the other way around, especially with every-thing that her arsehole ex was putting her through.

Chance had never liked Paul, he'd always had the feeling that he would leave his sister for someone younger, and it sucked that he had been right.

The night his sister had called him heartbroken with the news, Chance had wanted to kill the pig.

He had been happy when Carly had come home for a few months while he moved out.

It was during that time, Chance had promised Carly that he would be the responsible one, he let her know that he would take care of her for a change, and for a while he had been succeeding.

That was until Liz.

Perhaps Carly was right, maybe he really did need to start using his brain more when it came to women.

Carly had always accused him of thinking with his dick rather than his brain, and maybe she was right.

"No more." Chance vowed. It was time he grew up and thought about his future.

Hopefully Carly could sort this mess out, so he still had a future.

Rage filled Chance once more. There was no reason for

this woman to be doing this. Chance had to talk to Carly and find out what their plan was going to be, he couldn't sit by any longer.

Turning around, anger driving him, Chance opened the bathroom door and ran straight into another body. At first, he thought it was Carly or one of the kids.

"You know you could wait your turn..." The rest of his sentence was cut off when the blue eyes of a stranger met his.

Chance had no idea who this waif of a girl was in his arms, and he hated the fact that his cock started to harden the longer he stared at her, especially since he had just decided not to think with his little brain.

Her chestnut hair hung over his fingers where they lay on her bare arms. He had instinctively grabbed them to stop them from falling, but now he wished he had let her fall on her behind. Her skin was as soft as silk, and Chance had to reign in his desire to run his fingers along her arms.

Chance was just starting to gain his composure when her tongue darted out of her mouth and wet her lips.

"Sorry, I didn't know it was occupied." Her sweet voice washed over him.

That did not help him in the least.

The longer he stood holding her, the greater his need for her grew.

A smile played on his face as he looked down at her, and in that moment he remembered that he had had just chastised himself for falling for a pretty face and where that had gotten him.

The reminder of Liz and the shit he was in, coupled with his sexual need, had Chance snapping at her. For some unknown reason he believed that this woman had been sent here by Liz for some diabolical reason. Well he had news for the both of them, he was not going to give Liz any more ammo for her case.

"Who the hell are you and what are you doing in my house?"

Chance felt a little guilty for yelling at her when a slight blush rose to her cheeks, but not enough to apologise.

He had fully expected her to cower before him, which would in turn douse his desire for her but instead, she squared her shoulders and prepared for battle.

"Excuse me!" she bit.

Chance was not going to back down. He needed to do something to make sure this woman was kept at arm's length.

"You heard me. If you think you have come her to get something from me that will help Liz's case, you are sorely mistaken."

Chance had moved so that his face was close to the woman in front of him hoping that the anger he was feeling was evident in his eyes.

But all it did was raise her ire. He had to give her credit where credit was due. She was a tough one.

She was also a master actor. The confusion she was displaying almost had him convinced.

"Look, I have no idea who Liz is or what she would want from you. But as to who I am and what I am doing here, that is your *sister's* concern. And considering Carly is the one that hired me, and this is *her* house, I feel that I do not need to explain myself to you."

Chance didn't get the option to respond to the little spitfire as she ripped her arms out of his grasp and slammed the door to the bathroom in his face.

So the little minx knew who he was and still thought she would not have to explain herself to him, did she? And what the hell did she mean that his sister had hired her? Chance ran his hands through his hair as he made his way to his bedroom. The little spitfire in the bathroom was in for a rude shock but before then Chance decided that it was about time he had a talk with his sister. The last thing he needed around here at the moment was another woman messing up his life.

CHAPTER EIGHT

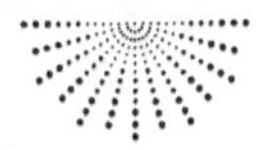

Turning to Charmaine, Paris let out a giggle.

"Are you tipsy?" Charmaine laughed at her.

Paris poked her tongue out at her friend. "You are not the only one who can have a good time, you know."

Charmaine raised her hands in defeat. Paris could tell she was just about to say something smart when something else caught her friend's attention. Charmaine let out a low whistle. "Come to Momma," she hissed.

Paris turned to see where her friend was staring, and she had to admit the two men that were walking through the crowd towards them were sex on a stick. She was shocked when they stopped in front of them and offered them drinks. Upon accepting the drinks, Charmaine invited them to sit with them.

At first Paris had been enjoying herself, but as the night went on she started to feel a little uncomfortable. The intensity in which the men kept looking at her with, seemed unnatural. Paris looked to her friend to see if she was feeling the same way, but Charmaine was oblivious to it all. She was talking the ear off of one of the guys, even though he was staring at her.

Paris shifted in her seat, it was then that it hit her, she knew *this man, she wasn't sure how she knew him, or where she knew him from, she just knew that she did know him.*

"Do you I know you from somewhere." Paris asked him over the music.

She expected him to answer her, instead he turned and kissed her best friend, passionately. Charmaine did not complain, she simply kissed him back. Paris was considering leaving, when the other gentleman handed her a drink.

Paris looked down at it, she all of a sudden didn't feel in a party type of mood.

"Thank you, but I think I will pass." She leaned forward and put the drink on the table.

The man beside her leaned forward and picked it up, placing it back in her hand.

"Come on now don't be a party pooper. Drink." Paris wasn't given a chance to think about it, he simply pushed the drink towards her mouth, effectively forcing her to drink. As she watched her friend make out with the stranger, Paris decided to push the doubts she was having to the bottom of her soul, she would not ruin her friend's night.

They had been looking forward to this night for a long time. Tipping her glass up she swallowed the liquor in one gulp, and no quicker had the liquid disappeared another glass replaced the first.

She did the same with this one, and as she finished it she could have sworn she heard the man beside her say, "that's a good girl." But she couldn't be sure.

She wasn't sure of much after that.

As they sat there watching the festivities around them her mind became fuzzy and even though she was sitting with Charmaine and the two men, she could not hear a word they were saying, all she could hear was the laughter of her friend, and the music that was pumping in the club.

Before long, Paris watched as Charmaine pulled out her room card as an invitation for the men to join them in their room. While

Paris felt excitement at the thought of having the two men to them-selves, the feeling of dread and foreboding was returning, and it overshadowed the moment.

The two men followed them back to their room, laughter and merriment followed the quartet, and then the moment came. Char-maine opened the door and entered the room, the men following her. Paris entered and took one of the drinks the men offered. The fun continued for a little. Noticing that they were out of ice, Paris grabbed the bucket and headed out of the room to get some more.

Paris waited for the ice machine to be free a strange wave of fear flowed through her, rushing back to the room, the sight of Charmaine and the men had her pausing.

Charmaine's dress had tears across her torso and blood covered her from head to toe, and even though she was smiling, the terror and fear that was evident in her eyes, terrified Paris.

Turning her head, she faced the men who were standing behind Charmaine, swirling black liquid in a glass, beckoning her to join them. But something was wrong, their faces were no longer that of the two men from downstairs, they were now twisted and contorted into evil personified.

Stepping back in horror, Paris tried to run, but her feet got tangled in the rug, and all she could do was scream as the men laughed and dragged her into the room. The sound of the lock clicking shut, was as loud as gunshot, sealing Paris into a room that she would never be able to leave.

Paris woke in her bed, sweat drenching her; the bed sheets had been twisted from where she had been tossing and turning. Her heart was pumping so hard she could feel it in her neck.

Placing her hand against her chest and trying to get her breathing back under control, Paris threw the sheets aside and made her way to the window seat that was starting to become her solace.

It gave her peace as she looked out at the night sky. Paris listened to make sure that she hadn't woken anyone with her nightmares, and then she turned her attention to the dream that had been haunting her for weeks.

The frustration that Paris felt each time she awoke from the nightmare, lay with the fact that once they entered the room, nothing became clear.

After all of this time and countless nightmares Paris still had no memory of what happened after she entered the room.

She knew that she had not been dragged into the room as the nightmare suggested, as she did vaguely remember one of the men stating that they were going to get more drinks before he disappeared.

But the feeling of foreboding had been real and the knowledge that Paris could not remember if he returned or what happened after only added to that feeling.

Besides the obvious issues, such as not remembering the night and the death of her friend, the other major thing that was bugging her, was the fact that she still could not for the life of her remember where she had known that guy from, but she was even more certain now that she *did* know him.

She had a feeling that he was in some way connected to her father and what happened.

If only she could remember.

As she had many a night before, Paris spent hours trying to figure out what happened, but when nothing came, she decided to curl up on the window seat and watch the sun rise. It was after all better than what faced her if she tried to go back to sleep.

Once awake Paris was always afraid to close her eyes in case the nightmare came back.

When she woke from the small amount of sleep she'd had against the window seat, the only thing she was concerned about was using the bathroom to freshen up before she got ready to find Carly.

Paris wanted to discuss a few things with her before they started their day, but the nightmares of the night before were still haunting and the last thing she wanted to do was meet her employer looking as bad as she felt.

Still tired and numb after her nightmare, Paris failed to notice the tall figure from last night leaving the bathroom. She was exhausted and trying to figure out how she was going to make it through the day without falling asleep when her body slammed into a wall of dripping wet muscle, and her senses instantly returned.

Her eyes remained glued on his muscular chest, but the moment his familiar deep, husky voice rolled over her, they moved to his face of their own accord.

Her breath hitched in her throat when she got a good look at him. His sandy blond hair lay in curls just above his ears, and his golden-brown eyes sparkled as the light caught them. A small smile played at the side of his mouth, showing a dimple at the end where it stopped.

She had seen the same smile on both Carly and her children. And the more she studied him, the more similarities appeared.

Stubble covered his square jaw, and when it twitched as

he bit down, Paris had the insane urge to run her hands over it. She wanted to see if it felt as strong as it looked.

She was highly aware of his hands on her arms, the skin where his hands sat practically burned at his touch, and the longer he continued to hold her, the more she wanted to feel that heat all over her body.

So much so she was worried that if he didn't move his hands soon, she would beg him to move them.

Paris swallowed hard, licked her lips and offered an apology for running into him. She was hoping that would take her mind off of his hands.

She wanted to introduce herself and put him at ease, but that was blown out of the water the moment he opened his mouth.

Paris was stunned, she could not believe he was being so rude to her, demanding to know who she was. From the resemblance to Carly, Paris could only assume that this was the infamous Chance, half owner of the ranch.

"Excuse me!" she asked, hoping that her snippy tone would make him reconsider how he was talking to her.

Who did he think he was, demanding to know who she was?

She knew she should tell him, she was in *his* house after all, but his demanding tone and snarky attitude brought out the spiteful side of her, which saw her being snarky in return. It was his own fault that she was less than pleasant.

When Paris had replied that she didn't have to explain herself to anyone but his sister, Paris felt a surge of pride to see his eyes widen in surprise a little. She got the feeling that the man in front of her was used to getting his own way. He didn't seem like the kind of man who was used to hearing 'no' from women.

What he didn't know though, was that Paris had spent a lifetime with men telling her what she could and couldn't do, demanding things from her and she'd had enough. With everything that was happening in her life, she was not willing to bend to anyone ever again.

Walking past him, Paris slammed the door shut and leant her back against it before shaking off the nervous energy and rushing from the doorway to the basin. She quickly splashed water on her face before grabbing the towel and wiping away the excess. When her face was dry, she looked at herself in the mirror. Her sleep deprived eyes stared back at her from a face that showed all the stress she had been feeling.

"You can do this. It is only for a few months. You just need to stay hidden for a few months and this job will allow that to happen." She sternly told her reflection.

Hanging the towel back up on the rack, Paris opened the door slightly, and after sticking her head out of the door to make sure the coast was clear, she made her way back out of the bathroom back to her bedroom. There, she got dressed. She slipped into something simple and comfortable. It was not as though she was teaching in a school, so she didn't expect that Carly would want her to dress that way. Looking at herself in the full-length mirror on her dresser, she checked herself once over, "well it's better than nothing," she mumbled.

Happier with the way she looked, Paris took a deep breath to steady her nerves before she headed to breakfast.

She was praying that Carly was going to be there, *alone*. She was in no mood to have another run in with Carly's brother, and they still had to discuss a few things – not only the details of her employment, but also the plans she had for the kids today.

The idea for the day's education came to her as she lay awake staring at the ceiling sometime in the middle of the night.

Entering the stunning kitchen that was something you'd typically see in a Home Magazine Ranch edition, Paris relaxed and sent up a silent prayer of thanks when she saw Carly sitting at the table alone, eating some cereal and going over some papers. She looked like she was in deep thought, Paris didn't want to disturb her as she looked as though she was concentrating on something important. The way Carly's brows were drawn together told Paris she was not overly happy with what she was reading, and every now and then, she would jot something on the papers.

Paris didn't mind waiting a little longer as it gave her a chance to gain her composure and wake up a bit more. The water had done little to remove the tiredness from Paris' eyes.

Paris looked around the kitchen and when her eyes landed on the antique looking kettle on the counter beside the stove she knew a sure-fire way to wake herself up.

Coffee.

Paris rarely drank the stuff, so when she did the caffeine would send her nerves into overdrive and she would often still find herself buzzing well into the night.

Walking over to the counter, Paris grabbed a cup of coffee and sat at the table across from Carly. She took a sip of her beverage and let the warm liquid rush through her sleep-deprived body. She waited for a few minutes expecting Carly would realise she was there, but when Carly turned to the next page and started writing notes, Paris realised that she was probably still unaware of her presence. Paris decided to sit and wait for Carly to acknowledge her, but the longer she waited the more nervous she became.

Finally, Paris had to say something.

"I hope I'm not disturbing you?" Paris said aloud, grabbing Carly's attention.

As Carly's eyes met Paris', they widened in surprise, Carly gave her a slight smile and she closed what she was reading.

"Not at all. It's great to see your friendly face this early in the morning. Did you sleep well?"

Paris wondered if Carly could tell that she'd had a rough night's sleep. Paris decided not to lie, just in case the evidence was clear. The last thing she needed was for Carly to hold any kind of suspicion towards her. So, she told the truth, well, a *slight* truth. "Not really, but you know what it's like sleeping in a new place, new surroundings and all that. The first few nights are always rough."

Carly nodded in agreement. "Don't I know it. There's no place like home, and there's certainly no place like your own bed."

Paris smiled. "It must help being here though, in a place you grew up in. This place must always feel like home." A feeling of regret passed through Paris. She wished she could understand what having a place like this felt like. Especially now, when she felt like she had no sense of home or place. She didn't know what the future held for her and just for a while she wanted to know what it felt like to have roots that anchored you safely to family.

Carly looked around the house and a nostalgic smile graced her face. Paris could only guess what she was feeling as she too took in the warmth of the wood lined walls, and the pictures that hung on every wall. Even the deer head and antlers that rested over the fireplace with such care denoted a house of family and love.

"You know, I've never thought of it like that, but you are right. This is the one place that I never feel out of place no matter how long I've been gone. I guess no matter how long I *am* gone this place will always be home. It's safe, you know what I mean."

Paris nodded, even though she hadn't had it often, she knew that feeling as she'd had it briefly when she'd lived with Charmaine.

Just thinking about her friend and the loss of safeness it

brought with it made the emptiness that was forever present grow deeper. Paris wanted nothing more than to scream. She had lost so much in so little a time.

Paris *needed* to find the truth of what happened that night; she knew her life would never feel safe again until she did.

Right now, she envied Carly her life.

Plastering a fake smile on her face, one that she would have to get used to wearing, Paris answered, "I know what you mean."

A calm silence settled over the breakfast table as both women became lost in their own thoughts. Paris wanted to ask more questions. She wanted to bring up the topic of the kids and payment, but she decided to leave that for Carly to bring up. The last thing she wanted was to seem pushy. Nothing had been decided for sure yet, and Paris was still worried that Carly could change her mind at any moment.

Thankfully, it didn't take her long. "Well I guess since we're here on our own, we should really talk business, shouldn't we."

"Well I was going to let you eat breakfast first." Paris laughed, happy that the subject was back in place.

"Meh, we can do that *while* we eat. Besides, once we get business out of the way, then we can talk pleasure." Carly smiled. Paris relaxed in her chair a little more as the realisation that this was going to go smoothly hit her.

The more time she spent with Carly the more Paris began to realise that she was someone that Paris could form a friendship with.

"Before we get talking money, I would like you to first explain what you have planned with the children today. You do have something planned right?"

Paris tensed a little, she was anxious that what she had planned was not going to be enough. What would she do if Carly was not happy with her ideas? Would she take back her offer? Paris' heartbeat picked up a few beats and she could feel her nerves taking over. This conversation was starting to feel like a test.

Carly must have realised that too, because she leaned across the table and tapped her hand. "Relax Paris, this is not a test. I am just curious to see where your mind is going and what kind of ideas you have. From there I will be able to determine how much you are going to be worth to me and we can come up with a figure."

Paris' excitement started to grow again. This was what she wanted to do with her life. Educate children and she couldn't wait to see if Carly liked her ideas.

"Actually, I do, but I want to run them by you first to see if it was okay."

Carly raised her eyebrows. "That sound ominous."

Paris smiled at Carly. "Not at all, I just wasn't sure how much the children already know or what you would be happy with me teaching them and I do know what you don't want them learning remember. Hence the checking in."

"Well now I am intrigued. Don't keep me waiting."

Carly leaned forward, placing her elbows on the table.

Paris laughed. "Now I have to make it sound exciting. Today I plan on teaching the kids a bit of Science and English."

A rush of pride entered Paris when Carly whistled, before saying, "That's ambitious of you. How do you expect do that *and* keep them from complaining?"

Paris was not the least bit offended by what Carly had said. It was a well-known fact that children of any age would complain and lose interest if there was *actual learning being* done. The aversion to learning appeared ingrained in them from birth.

"I have my ways. I guess that is one of the benefits of being a primary school teacher. I know that you have to make activities interesting to keep the kids engaged. If you let their minds wander for even a second, you have lost them."

"Don't I know it!" Carly laughed wryly.

Paris continued to spell out her plan to the woman in front her. Her hope was that Carly would approve of the activities. If she didn't, then Paris would have to go back to the drawing board and find another fun way to get the information across.

"Okay so first of all, for Science I thought I would take the kids for a swim in a lake or river, if there is one of course, *and* if it is alright with you." Paris asked.

Carly nodded that it was okay with her. "That sounds like fun, but please explain to me how you are going to teach them about Science while swimming."

Paris' smile widened. "This is where it gets tricky, but I have faith it will work. While they are swimming, I'm going to teach them about the water cycle and how the water moves around the Earth. I am also going to teach them about resources and the things that we have on this great land. I will keep it all simple and work it into the conversation as though it is a natural thing to talk about."

Carly was nodding in approval once more. "You *are* a tricky one. And the English?" she said, winking at Paris.

"Well that one I found a bit tricker, but I finally decided, that when we get home I will have them write up a story for you on what their day involved. I will tell them it is a fun way to retell events, I may even get them to read them to you as a bedtime story."

"I like you." Carly laughed leaning back in her chair. "Not only are you teaching my kids, but you are also eliminating a nightly argument we have on which story we are going to tell. You know if this works, I may just take you home with me."

Paris smiled at Carly's enthusiasm. It was always nice to be appreciated. "I'm glad you like it, now that I have your permission, I'm excited to get them up and going."."

"Alright, you've sold me, I have no doubt that you will do a great job. Now we have that part out of the way, let's finally talk wage. I was thinking about eight hundred dollars a week, including room and meals. Would that be suitable for you?"

Paris' eyes widened, she couldn't believe how much this woman was wanting to pay her. She wasn't expecting anywhere near eight hundred dollars, especially since Carly hadn't even done a background check on her or considering that she was paying Paris cash in hand. Paris wanted to argue the price, but she knew it would probably look strange. Most people would kill to earn that much.

"Are you *kidding*, it's a deal."

"Great, so all we have to do now is fill out some paperwork. I will need to grab your bank account details and then we can get the payments going in once a week."

Paris' heart stopped. She knew this was to be good too good to be true. She remembered asking Carly about being paid cash in hand when they first met, and although she had agreed, she had obviously forgotten.

Paris couldn't blame the woman. She had a lot on her plate at the moment, but that didn't help her out of her current situation, of all the things Carly had forgotten, why had it been the most important part of their deal.

Paris tossed up her options.

She could either leave and find somewhere else to find work, or she could try reminding Carly about their previous deal and see if she was still open to it.

Paris decided to go for the second option. She had nothing to lose as there were not many jobs around that would pay cash in hand and were above board. And there were definitely not many that allowed her to use her teaching degree. The only thing Paris could do was ask again and if Carly had changed her mind and said no, then Paris would leave. But until then, "about that, I thought we had decided…"

Before she could finish, Carly jumped in, slapping her forehead, she gasped, "Yes how silly of me. I forgot that it's going to be cash in hand. I'll pay you on a Friday, is that okay?"

Paris was about to answer but an angry voice boomed through the door.

"And why would you need to be paid cash in hand? What kind of scam are you running? Or better yet, what are you hiding?"

Paris' blood started to boil, she could not believe that this guy had the nerve to butt into their conversation. Her temper continued to rise as he entered the kitchen and grabbed a berry off the table, leaned against the counter and popped it in his mouth, giving her a smirk as he did so.

The jerk was not truly concerned about her hiding something, he was just out to get back at her for her actions towards him this morning. He had no idea how much trouble he was causing for her.

The fact that he had been so close to the truth had her heart racing. She had no idea why he was acting like a jerk towards her, but if she didn't do damage control soon, his not so subtle interrogation could ruin all her plans. The last thing she needed was for either of them to do a background search on her. God knows what they would find with the drama unfolding in Seattle. She was just about to offer an explanation to soothe his ruffled feathers, but Carly beat her to it.

"Chance, stop being a dick. I already know why she's here and I know the reason behind her wish to be paid cash in hand; this has to do with *my* children and *me*, and until you can keep your own personal life clean keep your nose out of mine."

Paris looked at Chance and gave him a smirk of her own. She didn't know what come over her, or why this man rubbed her the wrong way. She had no idea where her meek and mild side went in the company of this man, but she had to tone it down, while it may be okay to give as good as she got sometimes, she didn't want to rile him too much.

Carly might be on her side for now, but if her brother decided to go digging around, there was no telling what trouble he could bring down on her head. And she knew for sure that if Chance was to show real concern for his sister's safety, she would listen to him. From the small amount of time Paris had been in their company, she got the feeling that they were quite close.

And close families looked out for each other. Paris envied them their relationship. When she was little she had prayed that her brothers would stand up for her, that they would protect her, and for a while they had. But as the years rolled on, and she grew to be what her father wanted her to be, Paris soon came to realise that she meant no more to her brothers than she did to her father, she was simply an end to a means.

If only my family was normal.

Paris' attention was brought back to the present when a cup was slammed on the bench. He was pouring himself a cup of coffee, he seemed mad, perhaps she shouldn't have baited him, Paris thought miserably.

As much as he annoyed her, Paris would have to try and get a handle on her emotions around him, she just prayed that he would let it go this one time, but as her luck would have it, he didn't.

"You're the one who is always saying that we need to look

out for each other, and this is my way of making sure that *you* don't get taken for a ride. After all, you have to be careful what some people are teaching your children. You never know, she may be a criminal mastermind and could be planning to teach your children how to con people out of their money.

God, how was this man getting so close to the truth? Things were getting out of hand and fast, she needed to do something and quick. Paris got ready to reassure Carly that she only had good intentions when it came to her children, but the cloth flying through the air and hitting Chance in the head stopped her. Paris had to cover her mouth to hide the laughter that was now bubbling up.

"You're an idiot." Carly simply said to her brother.

"Well it's the truth, God knows what bad habits she will teach them." He muttered removing the cloth from his face.

Carly rolled her eyes.

"Well at least she will be teaching them Maths. And no-one can teach them any worse habits than you and your men did the last time I was here." She added, shooting him a glare.

It was Chance's turn to laugh. "Hey, I have already apologised for that. I have explained a million times that we didn't know they were there."

"Mhmmm," was Carly's only reply before she turned back to Paris.

"Look, please just forget about him, okay, this is between you and me. I'm fine with everything we've discussed, *and* I'm sure as shit fine with what you're going to teach my children. In fact, I can't wait to hear what hear about it at story time tonight. Now you had better eat something while you have the time, because the minute they are awake…"

As if on cue, the pitter-patter of little feet came rushing down the hall. Carly shook her head laughing, all the worry of the previous conversion was slowly disappearing and once again, the excitement Paris had felt when she first entered the kitchen filled her. Leo was the first one to barrel into the room, he headed straight into the muscular arms of his uncle before turning around to face the women at the table.

"What are we going to do today?" Nerada asked Paris, as she pulled a chair out and sat between her mom and her. Paris had been so entranced watching the man at the counter that she had missed Carly's daughter entering.

"Well that, my dear, is a surprise. I guess you'll just have to have breakfast before you get ready for a day out and about." Paris offered the young girl. Paris was rewarded with a smile in return.

"Oh yeah that sounds like fun." Leo squawked as he wiggled his way out of his uncle's arms before he joined the females at the table.

"You bet it's going to be." Paris answered them, choosing to ignore the man who continued to lean against the counter, watching her, she knew it was his way of trying to unsettle her.

As the children ate breakfast and chatted, Paris mentally went through the list of what she had to organise.

Slowly she began to relax a little, but not completely, how could she under the relentless gaze of the man who stood there just waiting for her to do something wrong?

Normally a person would be able to ignore his gaze, but her secret that rested just below the surface would not allow for her to let her guard down. Paris knew that she would have to be on guard while around these people. Paris had a hunch that once she got to know Carly better it would become easier for her let her guard down.

And Chance, well with him it was a whole different story, Paris had a feeling that he would be like a dog with a bone, and the moment he even sniffed out a hint of trouble he would pounce.

CHAPTER NINE

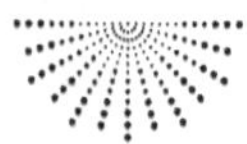

Chance growled as he walked out of the house behind the woman who had invaded his home. She was being followed by his niece and nephew. He had no idea why this woman rubbed him the wrong way, but she did.

Chance watched as Nerada and Leo showed the new nanny the lay of the land.

She was laughing and listening to them as they chatted about the adventures they were going to have.

It wasn't until they were halfway across the yard that he finally realised he hadn't moved from the bottom of the porch.

"Pull yourself together man." He berated himself.

The way he was acting it was as though he had never seen a good-looking female before.

Shaking his head at his own stupidity, Chance made his way over to the barn to get his horse ready for the day, trying to dispel any thoughts of the beguiling girl from his mind.

As he pulled Prahas from the barn and started to prepare him for the day, his friend, Bronx, came up beside him and whistled. "Who is *that?*" he asked, tipping his head towards

Paris and the children who were wandering off towards the river.

Chance had learnt from the conversation Carly and Paris had, in the kitchen that they planned to go swimming.

Chance turned his head to take in Paris once more, she was now holding the children's hands, and the sun was shining on her chestnut hair bringing out the highlights. Chance looked at his friend who was also staring at the trio; he had heard the interest in his friend's voice, and suddenly Bronx's question caused pure jealousy to rush through him.

Chance didn't understand where this feeling was coming from, he didn't want the girl and yet the thought of someone else taking an interest in her didn't sit well either.

Chance grunted, he knew she was going to be trouble.

"The new nanny," Chance bit off with a little more force than necessary.

If it had been anyone else but his best friend, they wouldn't have given two thoughts to the tone that had entered Chance's reply, unfortunately Bronx was the one who had asked the question, and therefore the tone did not go unnoticed. All Chance could do now was wait for the forthcoming questions.

Questions he did not know how to answer.

Bronx's eyes met his, narrowing as though they were trying to figure something out.

"Is she available?" Bronx asked innocently, turning to face the woman that had become a thorn in Chance's side.

Now not only was he going to have to fight this attraction towards her, he was also going to have to fight to keep his men's minds on the job. If his best friend had noticed how attractive she was, then it wouldn't take much for the other ranch hands to notice. Chance hadn't even considered what trouble she would bring among his men.

What had Carly been thinking hiring a woman such as her to come and work on a ranch full of horny men?

His eyes fell back on the woman as she continued her trek. Her hair was in a ponytail that reached her lush bottom. A bottom that was barely covered by the short shorts she was wearing. Her peach tank top clung to her toffee coloured skin, accentuating each curve as she walked. Another growl from deep inside of him formed and hissed out through his lips as the next words left his mouth. "She could at least wear clothes that fit her while she is here."

Chance groaned when Bronx looked at him and raised a questioning brow, and he knew he had just added more fuel to Bronx's already growing suspicion, but he couldn't help himself, Chance wondered what had possessed the woman to dress like that.

Didn't she know how distracting she looked?

How could she not know that she possessed a body that could drive men crazy? Hell, it drove him crazy. That clothing on anybody else, he wouldn't have been bothered, but for some reason on her it did bother him. It didn't help that all of his men were now staring at her.

"*No,* she's *not* available. Do you all hear that?" He said loudly, gaining the attention of all his workers. "The girl is off limits. My sister will kill any of us that give her cause to leave, so remove her from your minds and get it back on the job at hand," he ordered.

Chance knew he shouldn't have put so much feeling behind his statement, he had added the part about his sister hoping to quell any suspicions, but he knew it hadn't worked.

Bronx's, eyes turned back to him, boring into his soul, letting Chance know that he had caught the slip up.

Chance hoped like hell he would let it go, but as the next

words left Bronx's mouth, Chance knew he wasn't going to let it go without a few shots.

He wasn't surprised, nobody knew Chance like Bronx did, the pair had been friends since they were nine, and if the tables had been turned, Chance would have done the same. Bronx knew everything about him, and he also knew his moods better than anyone else.

"What's gotten into you?" he asked, knowing full well what it was.

There was no hope in hell that Chance was going to admit to having a thing for the new nanny, especially not after the last debacle.

"Nothing, nothing at all." Chance backpedalled, but when Bronx simply raised an eyebrow letting him know that he was not going to let it go, Chance continued, "trust me it is nothing. I learnt my lesson the last time. The last thing I need is another woman coming around here causing trouble where trouble doesn't need to be. We have a heap of work to get done if we are going to get the cattle ready to go to market next week."

Chance hoped that would appease Bronx for now, and when he simply nodded, Chance let out a breath and mounted his horse, but he should have known his friend better, Chance turned in time to see Bronx's grin.

"That's if your sister can smooth over the mess you made at the marketplace."

Chance flipped his friend off before replying, "You don't need to remind me what shit pile I placed us in. I'm sure as shit not looking forward to having to drive over ten hours just to find a place that will actually take our cattle, thanks to that little bitch."

Bronx chuckled and shook his head as he mounted his horse.

"You know, you if you want to solve all of your problems,

simply stop being so good in bed. Perhaps then the women you sleep with wouldn't go bat shit crazy for your loving. Shit man, I am starting to think your dick is made of gold, the way they act." Bronx added, shaking his head.

"God, please do not think of my dick." Chance added with a fake shudder for good course.

He got the reaction he had been hoping for, Bronx's humour turned to disgust. "Dude, too far," was all he gave back as a reply before he made his way out of the barn, with Chance hot on his heels.

Chance knew it was a low blow, but he had to get his friend's mind off what they had been talking about, and thankfully for now it worked.

Chance kicked his horse into a trot and soon he was riding side by side with Bronx. He hadn't been kidding with Bronx back in the barn, if Carly couldn't sort this mess out, he was going to have to take his cattle to the next state in order to be able to sell it, and that was the last thing he wanted to do.

The men headed out of the yards, following the path that the children and Paris had taken. They were headed over the west paddock today to bring in the herd grazing in its field.

Chance rode silently beside Bronx silently fuming over the situation that had been caused by him sleeping with the wrong woman. Why couldn't the women he found just be happy with what he offered?

If only it was his dick that they loved.

"What are you thinking so hard about?"

Bronx's question brought Chance out of his musing.

"It's not the size, or colour, of my dick the gold-diggers want you know, if only it were that simple. But no, it's always the size and colour of my bank account that matters to them. How in hell am I supposed to live my life if I am always wondering if it is me or my money they want?" Chance growled.

Bronx gave him a sympathetic look. On anyone else it would have pissed Chance off but, Bronx had been beside him during each and every failed relationship, when it turned out all the women wanted to do was trap Chance, so he knew that Bronx understood where his doubts came from.

Just once Chance wanted a woman to like him for himself and not fuck with his life just because he wasn't prepared to marry fakery. But that was never going to happen; every woman he'd met had an agenda of their own. Thinking about women and their agenda, his eyes turned back to where Paris and his niece and nephew were just disappearing over the ridge. He wondered what her agenda was. He just hoped that whatever reason she had for being here had nothing to do with money, and he hoped beyond hoped that she wasn't going to cause more drama.

He'd had enough of that on his own, he didn't need anyone helping him add to it.

With that last notion on his mind Chance kicked his horse in the side and quickened the pace so that he could keep the trio in his sight for as long as possible. He told himself that all he wanted to do was try and get a read on her, he just wanted to watch out for his family, but Chance knew the truth.

No matter how much he tried to fight it, he wanted this woman more than he had wanted any other, and that alone scared the shit out of him.

CHAPTER TEN

Darren Michaels picked up his phone and dialled the Seattle number Tommy had given him. He could not believe this was happening. It had taken him years to find out where his bitch of a daughter had run off too, so when a colleague of his had rang a few weeks ago from Seattle, talking about how proud he must be of his daughter's achievement, he had sent one of his best men over there to find out what was happening.

Turned out she had been living in the States all of this time and had even gone and got herself some kind of teaching degree. He knew she had done it as slap in the face to him, no-one in the family had ever worked an honest day in their lives, especially not for a pittance of a wage. It was her final way of shedding who and what she was. Well he had news for her.

Tommy picked up on the first ring, "Father..."

"Don't you father me, what the hell is happening over there? Why are you not home with Paris yet? Davenport is getting impatient, and you know what happens when rich men get impatient. If we lose this one Tommy, I will hold you equally as responsible as your ungrateful sister. Now why are you not on a plane home with her?"

Darren listened as his son gulped into the phone. He knew he wasn't going to like what he was about to hear.

"Well Pops, we did exactly what you said to do, we took away all of her reasons for remaining. I even left a note for her so that she would know that the only option she had was to come home with us. But…"

"But what?" Darren demanded.

"Well she did what Paris always does, she ran."

Darren had to take a minute before he answered, the rage that was boiling up inside of him. It was a rage that was dangerous, if he did not get a hold of it he would find himself making a decision that could jeopardise the whole operation, he needed a clear head for what came next.

How could this be happening? His daughter had disappeared once again.

"So, help me God, when she gets home, I'm going to take great pleasure in offering her to Davenport for all the trouble she has caused me."

Darren slammed his hand down on his desk as the rage continued to build. If he did not find Paris and soon, he would lose millions of dollars, this was the kind of con he waited his whole life to pull off, but the man in question would only deal with Paris. He had seen her picture in Darren's fake office the day he had come in, and that had set the current events in motion. *How could he have been so stupid?*

Darren picked up the offending photo in question and threw it at the wall, smashing the glass to smithereens. Darren's wife had been entering the study the moment the photo hit the wall, without saying a word she turned around and left again. Darren sat down at his desk with a sigh.

"I'm sorry Pops, I honestly thought she would come home with her tail between her legs. Especially now."

"What do you mean, especially now?" Darren asked his son. He was now sitting forward, his elbows firmly planted on the desk.

"Well you wanted her to have no reason to stay, and so we took away her life here. We offed her best friend, and made it look as though she had done it. She has no home, no friend and is on the run from the cops. The only way she will get out of it is if she comes home. But she ran."

Darren smiled for the first time since he'd started talking to his son.

"Dad, you still there?" Tommy asked through the phone.

"I'm still here." He answered as a plan started to form in his head.

"So, what do I do?"

"Nothing son, you do nothing."

Darren could hear Tommy pacing through the phone.

"But Pops."

"Tommy, everything will be fine. For now, I want you to stay put. Where are you staying?"

Darren wrote down the address, before addressing his son once more.

"Alright, do not do another thing until I get there; is that clear?"

"But what about Davenport?"

"Screw Davenport. Getting your sister back in the folds of this family is of the utmost importance right now. I am sure once she is here, we can convince Davenport to get back on board. Hell, I will sell your sister to him if I have to. For now, you are to wait."

"Got it Pops. See you soon."

Darren disconnected the call to his son, turned on his computer and booked his flight. Paris had no idea about the shit storm that was about to rain down on her head, and he couldn't wait to get her home and make her pay for the trouble she had caused in his life.

Getting up from his desk, he walked out to the kitchen to let his wife know what the plan was and to get her help in packing.

"Game on Paris darling." Darren hadn't felt this alive in years. It was time to get some revenge.

CHAPTER ELEVEN

Paris' heart smiled as she reached the river that Carly had told her about.

She wasn't wrong, it was beautiful. It was already bringing her peace.

The way the river meandered its way like a serpent slithering from side to side through the hills and down to its final resting place where it formed a large pool before continuing its journey. It was just perfect for what Paris had in mind. She could see herself spending a lot of time here, with and without the kids. It looked like the perfect place to do some thinking. Right now though, Paris had a job to do.

"Alright guys, this is where we are going to park ourselves for a few hours and finish up our lesson." Paris informed the kids as she placed the picnic basket under a huge tree that provided shade by the river.

The whole way down to the river, Paris had taught the kids about the water cycle and how important it is to the land they live on. At first the kids had groaned about the fact that they were learning something, but the more Paris explained how the water worked on the land they owned, the more questions the children had.

All of the questions led to them having a discussion about what water was, and therefore Paris was able to teach them that water was an element and what it was comprised of. Thankfully, by the time they reached the river the kids had been enthralled and saw it as an adventure rather than a lesson.

They asked questions as well as answering them enthusiastically. Paris was quite pleased with herself.

"Can we go for a swim first, before we do anymore learning?" Leo asked, already ripping off his clothes.

Paris laughed. "Do you know how to swim, or do you need me to come in?"

The look that crossed the little boy's face was comical. It was though she had just asked him the most offensive questions in the world.

"I am six years old, of *course* I can swim."

Paris put her hands up in defeat, her way of apologising.

"Sorry, I was just making sure." She offered him when he continued to look at her with offence.

"Uncle Chance taught us to swim when we were young so that we would never drown if we fell into the river or dam." Nerada added.

Paris smiled, the one thing she couldn't fault Chance Malloy on was how much he loved his family.

"Well that was very wise of him, wasn't it?" She added in recognition of the information she had just received.

Both children nodded, before they continued to strip down to their swimmers, and then proceed to enter the water, with screams of laughter at how cold the water was.

Paris smiled as she watched the children play; as the sun beat down on her she decided to get comfortable. Soon she sat in the shadow of the tree, thankful for the shade that was protecting her from the sweltering heat. There she sat, watching as the kids swam in the river, splashing and laughing, enjoying their childhood.

"Are you coming in soon?" Nerada asked.

Paris was seriously contemplating it as the heat from the Wyoming sun baked her skin even in the shade, warming her up from the inside. Beads of sweat had started to form, running down in between her breasts and the stickiness that she was feeling from the heat was becoming a bit much to bear.

Looking around, Paris noted that they were still alone, but she was just making up her mind when Chance and his men started to pass by them on their horses.

Paris hoped that they would not be noticed, and the men would just go on their merry way, but that was not to be, as the kids hooted and hollered, waving their arms to gain his attention.

Of course, they thought nothing of greeting their uncle, they were not the ones that had something to hide or felt uncomfortable whenever he was near. That was simply her problem.

He smiled and whistled letting them know that he saw them.

Paris prayed that the men would simply pass by and continue on with their work, but, as her luck would have it Chance swung his horse around and headed straight towards them.

The hat he was wearing did not hide anger she could see in his eyes and he was on her within minutes. Paris was confused. What did he have to be angry about? Carly said it was okay for her to bring the children here, and they could obviously swim, which he knew, as he had taught them.

Paris racked her brain trying to figure it out, but she wasn't left in the dark for too much longer.

Within second his horse was so close to her, that she could feel the sweat on its flanks with her arms.

She should have been scared with an animal this large near her, it had to be at least seven hands tall, but the control in which the mount had was evident in the way it stood still for Chance. It was obvious that the horse respected Chance, as he did the horse. She wondered if Chance had reared it up from a foal.

"Next time you decide to come out in this heat, have the sense to put on decent clothes." He hissed so that only she could hear.

Paris could not believe what she was hearing. Her mind was quickly taken off the beast next to her and was abruptly placed on the beast astride instead.

The way he was speaking made him sound like an old man. Who, in this century, complained about what women wore?

She was just about answer him when the kids cried out.

"Come for a swim, Uncle."

Chance turned to them and shook his head.

"Sorry rats, I have to get back to work, Bronx can't handle all the cattle on his own. Maybe another time."

Paris was pissed off now, knowing that the only reason he had come over here was to berate her about her clothing as though he had the right to.

Well she had news for him; she had promised herself years ago that she would never allow another man to tell her what to do, and what better way to keep that promise than to show this jerk just what she thought of his mandate.

Turning to the kids she placed a smile on her face, before saying, "it's okay, kids, your uncle can go and work. *We* will have *all* the fun."

She then turned back to Chance, a sly smile playing on her lips. She always liked the saying, don't get mad get even.

That is exactly what her line of thought was as she began to strip off the said clothing that he had a problem with.

If he had a problem with her clothing on top, he sure as hell wasn't going to like the bikini that she was wearing underneath.

Removing her top slowly, she began to reveal the pink halter style top with crisscrossing strings over her D sized boobs. For the first time in her entire life, Paris was thankful for her full breasts.

She made sure that as she pulled the top over her boobs she went slowly, just for show and when she was finished pulling her tank top over her head she flung it to the side, making sure to make a show of it.

A small amount of pride filled her when she heard a sharp intake of breath from the man in front of her. This allowed her to grow bolder.

Paris had planned on wearing her shorts into the river when she swam, but now, on principle, she decided to remove them, and she did just that, *slowly*.

Paris made a show of undoing the button on her shorts, and unzipping them, all haste gone of course. Then turning her back to the man who was driving her insane, and as she started to push them down over her hips and past her derriere, she made sure to give it a little shake, as though the shorts had gotten stuck. Then one leg at a time, she removed them before adding them to the pile with her shirt.

Now standing there in only her bikini, she started making her way to the river. Just as her toes touched the edge of the water, she turned to Chance, the genuine smile that played on her lips from the coolness of the water added to the statement she was making.

Paris was happy to see that she had struck a nerve, and that gave her the courage to say, "Well you'd best get going, all that work is not going to wait," and with that, she dove into the water to the sound of the kids laughing, along with the booming laugh of one of his men. She was a little embarrassed that she had forgotten they were not alone, and that kept her under the water a little longer than she had originally planned. It was his fault, whenever he was around, everything else around her seemed to just fade away.

Soon Paris emerged from her dive and stood up running her hand over her hair to remove it from her face. She felt the water from her hair run down her body. She was not trying to entice anyone as she had expected Chance to have stormed off, but when she turned back around, she was surprised to see him give his men the cue to keep going.

The man in the lead simply nodded then headed out with the others, his laughter continuing as he went.

Paris' heart sped up as Chance dismounted his horse and made his way to the river, removing his clothes as he went. There was a power in his stride, and the way he looked at her, had her body warming up once more. Perhaps this hadn't been such a great idea after all Paris thought to herself, as she lowered herself deeper into the water.

The children hooted and hollered as excitement filled their hearts at the thought of their uncle joining them.

Paris, on the other hand, her excitement had just turned to apprehension. That apprehension, along with something else, continued to grow as each new piece of skin on this man was revealed.

When he was just standing there in his boxer shorts, all sane thought left Paris' head.

"I thought you had work to do?" She asked, licking her dry lips, hoping that he would just go away. It was easy being brave when she thought he wasn't going to hang around.

"Nah, this looks like more fun," He drawled, sauntering to the river.

Paris watched as he dove effortlessly into the water and

resurfaced near his niece and nephew, just a few feet away. Thankfully the kids were keeping him occupied, jumping on him, trying to drown him. He of course was stronger than they were and soon he was throwing them around as though they were rag dolls. The kids loved it of course and Paris took his brief distraction as time to gain her composure, but it was soon destroyed when the children started swimming around by themselves, giving him the chance to speak to her.

Swimming up behind her, Chance wrapped his arm around her waist under the water, placing his hand along her ribcage, just under her breasts. From an onlooker's point of view, it simply looked as though he was standing behind her, watching the children play, but to her it was something different.

The places on her body where his skin met hers felt as though they were on fire, every nerve was alive, and butter-flies erupted in her stomach. It was a heady feeling knowing that he was secretly touching her while no one else would be the wiser. Paris was just starting to get her body under control when one of his fingers ran up under her bikini top to play with the underside of her breast.

Her bikini bottom pooled with her excitement, and she thankful that they were in the river as her whole body was once again hot.

She didn't think she could get anymore turned on, until he pulled her back, so she was practically sitting in his lap, his own excitement evident, then his hot breath whispered across her ear.

"You really should have thought twice before you threw down the gauntlet with me, the war is on."

Before Paris could answer him, Chance slowly removed his hand, deliberately making sure she felt every inch of it as it ran across her torso. The sensation he was creating across her body sent molten need rushing to her core.

What had she done?

Before she had gained her wits enough to reply, Chance had once again joined his niece and nephew who were now in the process of trying to drown him once more.

Paris could do nothing but stand there, her body still tingling from the encounter, as his words continued to play around in her head.

The last thing Paris wanted was to start anything with anyone. All she had wanted to do was prove to him that he could not control her, instead she had unleashed a side of him she was not sure she was ready for.

What the hell did he mean by the war was on?

What have I done?

CHAPTER TWELVE

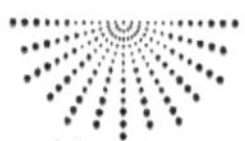

A month had passed since the day in the river, a month of pure hell and heaven mixed in one. Paris and the children had fallen into a nice routine of having fun while learning. Carly was impressed by how much her children had learnt over the last month, and even though Paris had considered moving on to save any more attachments, Carly's offer for a permanent nanny job with her was too tempting.

Paris' life had fallen into an easy rhythm. Each day was spent with the children, wandering the farm and learning new and fascinating things, and on the days when they could not get out of the house due to the rain or storms, Paris made sure that the lessons she planned were as equally exciting and stimulating. Each night at the dinner table the children filled their mother in on their adventures and what they had learnt. Both their spelling and Maths had improved, and they were no longer complaining about learning. In fact, they often bugged Paris about what they would be learning next.

The friendship between her and Carly had also grown. Each night, after the children had quieted down for the night the girls would take a drink out onto the veranda where they would gossip as though they were teenagers in high school. They shared their past experiences and their future dreams; Carly talked about the hurt and betrayal her husband had forced on her, and the how she would love to find another to heal hers and the children's hearts. She also confided that she was afraid of how the whole situation would affect the kids growing up. Paris shared only snippets of her childhood and her life, up until the murder, afraid of giving too much away.

"My dream for the future is no different to yours though." Paris admitted one night.

Carly turned and looked at her.

"Then why do you plan to move on?" Carly had asked her.

Paris thought about one of the first conversations they'd had in the weeks after Paris had started here. She remembered telling Carly that she was not sure when she would move on, but that she would.

"What has one got to do with the other?" Paris quizzed turning to face her friend.

The knowing smile she gave her made Paris' heart ache. It was the same smile Charmaine use to give her when she thought Paris was being daft.

"Come on Paris,"

"Come on Paris, what?" she asked turning to face Carly more fully. Paris truly had no idea what Carly was talking about. How did her staying here have, in anyway, anything to do with her future? Carly would be going home soon and once the kids and Carly were gone, there would be no reason for her to stay.

With that thought Paris felt a wave of sadness she could not explain wash over her. Turning back to face the farm, Paris looked up into the night sky and tried to forget the ache that was trying to settle in her heart.

"Alright, but just promise me you will keep your heart and your mind open to love. Wherever it may show up."

Paris smiled into the night; her friend was turning out to be a romantic. She was just about to answer when the farmhands walked across the yard towards the bunk houses. Bronx was at the head of the pack, and when he saw them sitting on the veranda, he gave them a wave. Paris waved back, then turned to Carly to answer her, and she was just in time to see the blush that had risen on her cheeks.

All of Carly's previous comments became clear.

"Only if you promise to do the same." She answered in reference to Carly's last comment.

Carly turned wide eyes to Paris ready to argue the point, but Paris raised her eyebrows in a knowing gesture, stopping the denial in its tracks. Carly turned to face the bunkhouse, before answering.

"It's just not that simple."

Paris lent into her friend and bumped her shoulder against hers, before stating.

"It never is. But the worthwhile things in life never are."

As the nights wore on, Paris became more comfortable, not only in her position as a teacher and nanny for the children, but in the life, she was living. Carly's openness and acceptance of what Paris had shared about her life thus far, lead to a feeling of calm, then the unimaginable happened.

The warm night air, along with the whiskey she was drinking warmed Paris to the core. Today had been tiring. She had spent the day walking the trails on the farm, teaching the kids more about the eco system and how all living things work as one.

They had hiked all day, Leo and Nerada were that worn out that they almost fell asleep at the table.

"It has been a while since I saw the kids that worn out." Carly commented, breaking into Paris' thoughts.

Paris laughed.

"Charmaine used to always say that the best way to send a child home was tired. That way the parents always knew that they'd had a great day. I guess she was right."

Paris leaned back into the rocking chair and smiled into the night. It was nice to remember the good times she'd had with her friend. Even now she could see the smile on Charmaine's face as she had imparted those words of wisdom on Paris when she first started teaching. Everything she had learnt and knew about teaching Paris had learnt from her.

As Paris looked up at the stars she wondered if her friend was up there keeping an eye on her.

"Who is Charmaine?" Carly inquired innocently.

Paris jerked her head up from where it was resting on the back of the chair.

"What?" She asked not sure she had heard the question right.

Carly looked at her with concern. "Charmaine, who is she? You have never mentioned her before."

Paris' heart was beating so hard she was sure Carly could hear it.

As Carly sat staring at Paris waiting for an answer, Paris knew she had two choices. She could either lie to Carly and give her the simple answer, or she could take a chance and finally let someone in to share her pain.

"Paris, it *is* okay to let people in sometimes." Carly offered, thinking that it had something to do with Paris' ex.

It was in that moment that Paris decided to give Carly half the truth. Paris wanted someone to know how important a person Charmaine had been to her, and Paris could not find it in her heart to make the importance of their friendship less than it was.

"She was my best friend, my confidant, my sister." Paris answered truthfully, before downing the rest of her drink.

"Was?" Carly pressed. Paris wasn't surprised that the word was hadn't passed her noticed.

Before she continued, Paris placed her drink on the table beside her and then walked over to the railing. Looking out into the darkness Paris took a deep breath for the courage it would take to say the next part.

"Yes was. She died." Paris turned around to face

Carly. She was sitting in her seat he legs wrapped underneath her and her hand was over her mouth.

"Oh Paris, I am so sorry. What was she like?"

A small smile rose on her lips as she thought about the best way, she could describe Charmaine.

"She was the ying to my yang." Carly laughed. Paris pulled herself up on the railing and sat with her back against one of the pillars as Carly joined her there.

"Charmaine was one of those people who knew how to make everyone feel special. I met her on my first internship for my teaching degree. She was actually my mentor, and when she heard that I was going to have to move from my current location she offered me the spare room at her place. And we become inseparable. She reminds me a little of you actually." Paris looked at Carly who was smiling.

"How so?" She asked.

"Well she was easy to talk to as well."

"Would you tell me more about her?" Paris thought about it for a split second before she nodded.

"I would love that."

Both Carly and she returned to their seats, Carly topped up their whiskey and the next hour was spent sharing stories of Charmaine's and her life. There were tears of joy and laughter, and there were tears of sadness.

"She was simply amazing." Paris ended taking the last sip of her drink.

"Well I concur, from what you have told me tonight, she was a woman to be reckoned with. I don't know how you consider her like me though. She was fierce."

Paris looked at her new friend, was she serious?

"Are you serious?" Paris couldn't help her thoughts escaping through her mouth.

"Well it's true." Carly pouted.

"Carly Malloy, you listen to me and you listen good. You *are* a force to be reckoned with. I mean just look at the way you handle your children, your brother and your crappy ex-husband. Anyone would be lucky to have you in their lives. And I will personally kick the arse of anyone who disagrees with me."

A slight blush rose on Carly's cheeks at the praise. "Well you're not a bad egg to have on one's side either." She joked.

Paris laughed and poured herself a little more whiskey.

"I think this will have to be the last one for me." She giggled starting to feel a little lightheaded. She had to admit it had been good talking about her friend.

Paris promised that Charmaine's memory would live on forever, even if she had to tell everyone about her.

"There is one thing I want to ask, and you don't have to tell me if you don't want to."

Paris waited, she expected Carly to ask her more about how she ended up here instead of teaching, but the question Carly asked was like a punch in the gut.

"How did she die?"

Paris' eyes started to water, she considered lying, but she would not dishonour her friend like that. Downing her drink once more, hoping to numb the pain that was going to come with her answer, Paris finally spoke.

"She was murdered."

Carly gasped. "Oh, Paris I am so sorry, I didn't know. I never would have…"

"It's alright, it was a while ago now." She lied.

"Did they ever find her murder?" Carly continued.

Paris' mind was screaming at her, screaming the word 'no' over and over again, screaming at the injustices that existed in this world. But she couldn't answer that way of course, so she had to lie once more.

"Yes, about a month after, it turned out to be an ex that had been stalking her."

"Oh Paris. I am so sorry."

So was she.

She hated knowing that she had lied to her new friend, but what could she say, 'No Carly they have not caught her murderer as they think the person who murdered her is sitting across from you, living in your house and teaching your children.' That would go down like a lead balloon.

Paris knew that she hadn't killed Charmaine, but until she could prove who was behind it all, then she was the prime suspect.

Paris was going to lose it, and she didn't want her friend seeing that.

Clearing her throat, Paris put her glass on the table and stood.

"Well I think that is all the drink I can handle for one night. I had better get to bed, otherwise your rugruts will run circles around me tomorrow." She let out a tiny laugh hoping to lighten the mood. It didn't work of course.

Carly rose from her chair and engulfed Paris in her arms.

"I am always here for you." She whispered before she let her go and walked past her into the house.

Paris couldn't stop the flood of tears that poured down her face.

"I really hope so." She whispered, because Paris knew that she would need all the friends she could get when the shit storm that was heading her way finally caught up with her.

CHAPTER THIRTEEN

From that night on things changed between Carly and her, they become closer, as though their troubled pasts and pain drew them together. It was a sisterhood of understanding.

The children had become like another part of her, and she loved them as if they were her own niece and nephew.

Everything was perfect.

Well almost everything was perfect.

There were just two things in this world that still caused her trouble. As she lay in bed looking at the celling, on warm summer night she contemplated the issues that she was facing.

The first issue that had been bugging her for weeks, since the night on the porch actually, was that Paris still had no idea if anyone had been named as Charmaine's murderer, she was still too scared to watch any newscasts, afraid that it would only confirm her fears that the authorities would be looking for her.

Every night when the family would sit down, she worried

that it would be the night the family would sit in front of the television and see her face scrawled across it. But as luck would have it, it turned out the Malloy's were not much of a TV family. Most nights everyone was too tired from their daily activities and would head off to bed, not long after dinner or after a nightly chat on the veranda.

She was not naive however, and she knew it would only be a matter of time before the truth came out.

She just hoped it was at a time when she had concrete proof on what happened, and she could clear her name. But that was a whole other issue, no matter how many dreams she had, or how much meditation she did, Paris was still no closer to remembering all that happened that night and with each night, the nightmares continued, and yet only small aspects of that night were coming out slowly.

All was not lost though, one of the things that had come back was that she finally remembered that after the guy had come back with the drinks, they had continued to party. Paris also remembered remarking on how the drinks that round had tasted different to the round before. The guys had just laughed it off and Charmaine had told her to relax. Paris now knew that the drinks had been laced with something that was designed to knock them out. It was designed to knock them out and make them forget.

From then on, there were only snippets of memory, some that Paris prayed were not real.

Snippets such as those of her friend begging them to stop, of Paris laying on the couch unable to move as she watched them take her friend one at a time. But after that, there was nothing, it was all black.

No sound.

No visual.

Nothing.

The actual murder still remained a mystery. She could not go to anyone or tell them the truth until she at least had a plausible explanation to go with. Just telling the police that they were drugged by two guys, who she couldn't describe or name, and who murdered her friend, but she couldn't say why, sounded preposterous even to her own ears. Paris still hadn't turned on her phone, she was afraid that if she did, they would be able to track her somehow. In reality, besides Charmaine and the police there was no-one that really would have texted her anyway.

The second thing that was giving her trouble was Chance – the ranch owning, horse riding cowboy who had made it his mission to drive her crazy.

Ever since the day at the river, every opportunity he got he was either passing judgement on everything she did, or he was whispering innuendos in her ear while manoeuvring his body into positions that would be guaranteed to make her crazy with need.

Paris had no idea what his game was, but whatever it was, it was driving her crazy. Not the mental type but the sexual type.

Every time his body was near, and his masculine scent invaded her nose, her hormones went wild. She had never considered herself the type of woman who was driven by her basic needs. But over the last few weeks she had lost count of how many times she had wanted to kiss him or reach out and touch him when he was near, but he was smart. He knew she wanted him, but he also knew that she would never act upon that need in front of his sister and her children, so he always made sure to make a subtle pass at her while they were nearby.

At first Paris had thought it was her in particular that he'd had a problem with, but while Carly and she had been on the porch one night the truth had come out.

"What's up with your brother?" Paris had asked. She tried to keep her question as light as possible. The last thing she wanted was Carly thinking there was anything going on.

When no answer was forthcoming, Paris dared a look at her friend. Carly was simply sitting there with her eyebrows raised.

"What?" She asked feeling self-conscious.

"Why the sudden interest in Chance?" She laughed.

"Is there something I should know? Not that I am complaining, I would love to have you as a sister."

Paris spat out her drink at that comment, which brought on laughter from her friend.

"God no, I was just curious if is only me he dislikes so much or is it woman in general?"

Carly gave her another quick look and smirk before she answered.

"Don't take it personally. And he really doesn't hate woman as such."

"Sure, could have fooled me." Paris added, then groaned. *Why couldn't she keep her mouth shut?*

Carly simply laughed again. "No really, Chance used to be so carefree and trusting."

"What happened?" Paris had asked.

"It wasn't so much as one big thing happening, it was more like a lot of little things actually."

"And by little things, you mean woman, right?" Paris asked.

Carly simply nodded. "You got it. You see Chance has never really been lucky in love. In fact, you could say it is the complete opposite. Every time he dates someone it always ends in disaster before it can even get serious."

"You're joking right?" Paris asked bringing her feet up underneath her suddenly interested in what Carly had to say.

"No, I'm not really. For instance, let's discuss why I am

down here. You would have heard by now about the trouble his last fling has caused," Carly sighed.

Paris nodded. She had caught the end of an argument that had transpired between Chance and said woman, when she had rocked up here one day, begging him to take her back.

As Paris stood in the shadows and watched the interaction, she had wondered where the woman's pride was. It was obvious that Chance was not interested. She had started to feel sorry for the woman.

That was when things got really interesting and all the sympathy that Paris felt for the woman went out the window. Chance was in the process of turning her down flat once more, but instead of begging again the woman become so spiteful that Paris doubted she had been sincere in the first place.

That day, Liz had threatened Chance. She warned him that losing his licence to sell meat at the Cody Marketplace was going to be the least of his trouble.

When that got no rise from Chance, Liz then threatened to drag his name through the mud, so much so that the entire ranch would be ruined.

"Not even your sorry little sister will be able to bail you out of this one Chance." She had spat.

It was then that Paris found out why Carly was here, she had spent the last month trying to undo what this harlot had done. Paris felt the overwhelming need to protect her friends wash over her and she wanted nothing more than to rip out this bitch's hair. But she knew Chance would not appreciate her knowing his affairs. So she stayed quiet.

"Oh yes, wasn't she pleasant." Paris answered, brining herself back to the present. She wasn't worried about letting Carly know she'd heard of the encounter, it wasn't like Carly would accuse her of eavesdropping.

"Well let's just say she wasn't the first to try this crap on Chance. His whole life has been spent dating women who have set out to deceive and trick him. And every time he had met someone, it turns out they never want him, they only want the money."

"That's sad," Paris stated. She really did feel bad for him. She wanted to argue with Carly and tell her that she was being a pessimist, but if her family history had taught her one thing, it was that people did horrible things for a get rich quick scheme.

Why did these women have to be so shallow?

These types of women made it hard for those women in the world who were only after love and family.

"How come *you're* still so trusting? Surely you had the same problem."

Carly laughed. "Actually, I didn't. As far as anyone has ever known, the ranch belongs to Chance and Chance alone. We decided to do it that way to stop the gold-diggers coming after me; we never thought in a million years that they would be after him as well. I know it's not fair, but truthfully, I am happy we did do it that way because if my husband even suspected I owned this ranch, he would take me for half of everything."

"It still sucks that it has to be done at all."

"I can vouch for that."

That conversation had happened a little over a week ago, it had allowed Paris to look on Chance differently.

She felt sorry for him, she now understood why he liked to keep people at arm's length, and why he had been so suspicious of her to start with, but what Paris was still having trouble understanding, was how he could have fallen for Liz's crap in the first place.

Paris had seen straight through her crap the times she had been here. Her father and Liz had turned up at the ranch twice more, after the night she had tried to bribe chance into taking her back, at Carly's bequest. She was trying to iron out a solution that would make the harpy happy without giving her what she wanted. Carly had confided that she hated every moment she'd had to spend with her, trying to placate the gold digger. Paris didn't blame her.

Paris had run into Liz on two of those accounts and even though she hadn't known who Paris was, Liz had shot daggers at her. Paris knew her type, she was the type of person that would not let anyone, or anything stand in the way of what she wanted and what she wanted was Chance and this ranch.

That was a woman Paris did not want to get on the bad side of. Starting anything with Chance would be doing just that. The last thing Paris needed was to draw any unwanted attention to herself. No man was worth that.

Paris couldn't lay here thinking about Chance or her situation any longer. Throwing the bed sheet off of herself, Paris climbed out of bed, walked to her the chair in the corner and chucked on her floral dress that she'd planned on wearing tomorrow. Paris slept in the nude, so she didn't worry about putting on any underclothing as it would only be clothes she would have to remove when she came back inside. Once she was clothed somewhat, Paris made her way outside.

The heat of the night made it so that she didn't need a jumper.

Leaving the house, Paris made her way across the veranda, and to the top of the steps. She wasn't going to go far; she simply wanted to go and sit in the gazebo that called out to her every night from her window seat and stare at the night sky. Ever since she was a kid, Paris had turned to the night sky for answers. She had always imagined that stars were her guardian angels who could offer her guidance in her life. Now she liked to think of Charmaine as being part of them.

Walking down the stairs, Paris sighed at the refreshing feeling once her hot feet sunk into the cool grass; she had opted against putting any shoes on, as she wanted to feel the ground beneath her feet. Being out here in the middle of the night made her feel young again; young and carefree.

With a smile on her face, Paris walked through the yard, until she reached the gazebo. It wasn't very large, but it did house three small benches that attached themselves to the walls, and three doorways with steps that lead up to the centre. The walls consisted of six straight pillars that connected to a simple frame at the top. Paris congratulated the genius that decided to put this here.

The gazebo offered the perfect place to stare up into the heavens. Its open top and placement on a slight hill made you feel as though the sky was within your reach.

Walking slowly up the steps, Paris looked around for a place to sit, she thought about sitting on the bench, but she wanted to be as close to the sky as possible, so she perched herself on the railing, leant her head back and stared up at the sky.

For the first time in a long time, Paris wished upon the stars above.

She wished that they would help her understand what happened to her friend.

But most of all she also wished for more willpower when it came to Chance, because God knows she needed it.

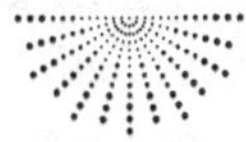

CHAPTER FOURTEEN

Chance smiled a small sly smile when he saw the figure leave the veranda he was currently sitting on and pass across the lawn to the gazebo.

"Just go inside Chance, you don't need another headache." He berated himself.

Chance was just about to go inside and give Paris her privacy but the moment he saw her in the moonlight, the lust that she had been evoking inside of him for the past month had him heading towards her instead. He knew it was a mistake, but it was as though his feet had a mind of their own.

At first the lust he had felt for her the day he had run into her outside of the bathroom had been easy to control. But then the day down at the river had occurred.

Chance had been angry at the way his men ogled her, he had only gone over to her to tell her to make sure she wore more clothes. The last thing he had needed was for his men to be distracted, especially with the amount of work they had to do to get the stock ready earlier because of Liz's interference in his sale.

That had been the plan, but the minute she had stripped down to her bikini, all the anger he had felt for the way his men had looked at her had washed away, and it had been replaced with an all-out need – a need to possess every part of her delicious body.

And that need had only increased the moment he'd felt her satin skin beneath his palms accompanied by her lush derriere pressed against his manhood. He knew she'd felt it too, his hand had been placed just below her breast and he had felt her heart beating erratically. If the children had not been in the water that day, he was sure he would have taken her then and there.

He hadn't wanted to let her go, but the moment he had felt his manhood stirring, he knew he had to put some distance between them. But the distance didn't help, seeing the water run in rivulets over the pastel skin of her neck set his blood on fire, he knew he was in trouble, he wanted her and he had a feeling that the only way he was going to get her out of his system was to have her. But that was the last thing he needed at the moment. But then again, when had he ever done what was best?

That had been a month ago, and ever since, Chance had been waging a silent war on her will. He took every opportunity he could to move his body close to hers, touch her, whisper in her ear and in every way, let her know that he planned to have her. He had to give her credit; she was holding off his advances quite well. Perhaps she didn't want him after all he thought as he walked across the yard. Well tonight he was going to find out one way or another.

Chance's feet had taken him to the gazebo while his mind wandered to everything he wanted to do to her. He couldn't put his finger on why he had to do this; he just had a gut deep feeling that sleeping with Paris would not be the same as all the other women he had bedded.

No, Paris was going to be something else.

What that something else was, he could not decide.

Leaning against one of the posts of the gazebo just to her right, he simply watched her admire the stars for a bit. But the moment she closed her eyes and leaned her head back, exposing her throat and chest in the glow of the moonlight, Chance had to make a move.

"Beautiful," he said in a low, gravelly voice.

Paris' eyes flew open and she turned to face him; the way her eyes widened from surprise had him wanting to draw her in close. He waited patiently to see if she would run, or if she was going to stick around. He didn't move, he simply continued to lean against the pole and watch her.

He could see the indecision play out on her face, part of him wanted her to leave and go into the house, and part of him wanted her to stay.

Chance watched as her eyes darted back to the house, and then up to the sky. She took a deep breath and then answered. Her decision made.

"Yes, they are. I can't believe how wide open the sky is out here."

That was all the invitation he needed.

Walking forward, Chance stood in front of her. He was done playing games. "I wasn't talking about the stars," he stated simply. He smiled when she swallowed deeply.

"Chance, I...." she tried. But he was not going to let her run this time.

"Do I make you nervous?" He asked, stepping closer. He knew phrasing it the way he did would not allow her to back down. One of the things he had come to learn about Paris over the last month was that she hated having him be right about anything, and she sure as hell hated it when she thought he was being condescending to her. Her pride would not allow her to back down from him now.

"No." She lied, while turning back to look at the stars once more.

He knew it was her way of dismissing him, hoping that he would somehow back down. But there was no-one here to save her tonight. Tonight, she was his.

"No, then I guess you won't mind me doing this." He whispered before he walked between her legs and pulled her against him.

That got him the reaction he wanted. The moment her core hit his stomach, her eyes flew back to his, her tongue darted out of her mouth and he could see her pulse racing in the base of her neck. She might say that he didn't make her nervous, but her body told a whole other story.

"Chance, I don't think this is…."

He knew exactly what she was going to say, but he was not going to give her the opportunity to talk her way out of this one.

Leaning forward, he captured her mouth with his own, effectively cutting off any further arguments that might pass through her lips. His lips continued their assault on hers, until her felt her finally relax against him.

Chance was further pleased when her arms wrapped around his neck and she started kissing him back. He could still feel the hesitance within her, fighting for some semblance of control. He knew what she was feeling because he was feeling the same thing.

"Don't think, just feel," he encouraged, both to himself as well as her as he kissed a path down her neck.

He knew the moment he had won her over, her head lolled back, and a moan escaped her lips. There was no turning back now.

Chance knew he had to slow down or he was not going to make it, his jeans already felt as though they were ten times too small for him, he wanted to take her in his bed, or at least somewhere that wasn't out in the open as they were now, but the woman in front of him wasn't allowing him any time to think, she was driving him wild.

"Chance," she begged as she rubbed herself against him.

He gave a slight chuckle at her eagerness, it looked as though they were going to do it right here, in the gazebo. He had to admit, it had always been a fantasy of his, that fantasy played out in his head as he reached down and ran his hand up her legs towards her core. This earned him another moan from her lips, and she wrapped her legs around him, anchoring herself there.

Chance's hands were soon at the junction of her thighs, she was bare underneath the dress, Chance moaned, his erection once again pressed painfully against his jeans.

"God woman, do you ever do anything normally?"

Chance's voice sounded husky even to his own ears. He looked into her face expecting some kind of snarky reply back, but he wasn't even sure she'd heard him. Her head was still resting on the pole behind her and her eyes were closed. Her hands were resting on his and the only indication she gave was a slight squeeze, of her hands on his, letting him know she was getting impatient.

Chance had the insane urge to see her eyes in that moment. Moving one hand away from her core, and brining it out from under her dress, he brought it up to her face. He gave a slight smile when she groaned at the loss of his heat.

"Look at me." He ordered, bringing her head forward away from the pole.

Paris slowly opened her eyes, and the lust that filled them, making them smoky with need, almost had him losing himself.

Chance needed to gain control of this situation and fast. "That's better," he replied, as he ran his thumb along her jaw and up over her bottom lip.

Paris took his thumb into her mouth, sucking it hard as he sank two fingers deep inside of her. Her eyes started to close once more, as she rode his fingers, the rhythm of her sucking his thumb, but he would not allow it.

"Do not close your eyes, I want to see every emotion on your face as you come." He hissed.

A moan was the only answer he received, but she did as he asked, she kept her eyes focused on his as he continued on his mission.

Her moans got wilder with the movements of his fingers, and the more she rode his fingers, the more he needed to be inside of her.

Reaching down between them with his other hand, he released himself, but the moment he had shifted his focus her eyes had once more shut and she head was once again leaning back against the pillar.

"Paris…" He had to say her name a little louder and stop moving his fingers to gain her attention. It worked, her head flew forward and her eyes opened, shooting daggers at him. He was right, she was a spitfire for sure.

"God, why did you stop?" she complained, digging her nails into his back.

Chance gave her a cocky smile before he answered.

"Because I need you to know that if you wish to stop this, now is the time." Chance knew that in the throes she had been in moments before he could have taken her with no fuss, but that was not who he was. He needed to hear the words.

The look she gave him was not one he had been expecting. He had been expecting her to come to her sense, to be honest, but instead she gave him one filled with the promise of death if he stopped. Her words only clarified that feeling.

"I am warning you now, Chance, if you do not finish this now, I *will*.

Chance chuckled before answering, "Well who am I to deprive a woman of what she wants."

This was said with one more thrust of his fingers, once again eliciting a moan from her. Chance continued to pleasure her, until she was once again at the heights she had been before. With one final thrust he pulled his fingers out and replaced them with his member.

This time the moan that greeted the air was from them both in unison.

Chance had never had someone fit him as well as Paris fit him. She enveloped his penis like a glove; it was as though her body was made especially for him.

That was the last coherent thought Chance had as Paris started to ride him. She rode him as though she had been born to the saddle, and with each sway of her hips against him, his passion for her grew wilder.

Within minutes they both reached their climaxes, screaming out into the night air.

When they had both come back to Earth, Paris rested her head against his shoulder and whispered, "That was amazing."

Chance didn't have words just yet for what he was feeling. He had slept with his fair share of women, but nothing had ever compared to what he felt here in this moment.

"You still with me Champ?" Paris asked when he didn't reply straight away.

Chance grunted when she poked him in his side, when he still didn't answer.

"That was nothing, Sugar, I have the night to show you the stars."

And that was a promise Chance planned to keep. He had already crossed the boundary with her, he might as well make it worthwhile.

CHAPTER FIFTEEN

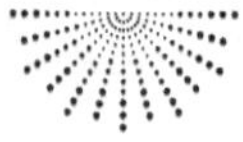

Chance hadn't lied.

That was the only thought that kept on repeating itself over and over in Paris' mind.

Chance hadn't lied.

After their rendezvous in the gazebo, he had taken her out to the loft in the barn where they spent the rest of the night exploring each other's bodies. Paris had never before experienced sex like she had with Chance. He seemed to know her body more than she did. He knew exactly where to touch her and how much pressure to apply to drive her crazy. And he also seemed to know without words that she was not the type of girl that liked it sweet and loving.

Paris loved sex wild.

Wild and free like she wanted to be.

Paris had expected the sex to calm down about the third time, but it hadn't. She had lost count of how many times and how many positions they had accomplished throughout the night.

But it had come to an end at some point and now it was three in the morning and they were laying in each other's arms staring at the sky through the roof opening of the musty barn.

Paris had expected them to head back into the house once Chance had had his fill; instead he seemed content to lay there with her. He was currently running his fingers along her back lazily, raising goose bumps there. He was giving her the indication that he was in no hurry to end their time together. They hadn't said anything to each other in the last few minutes, both just happy to lie there and bask in the love they had just made.

But the longer she lay there warm and safe in his arms, Paris' mind floated to what could be.

Over the last month, Paris had come to the realisation that it would be so easy to fall in love with this charming cowboy. When he wasn't antagonising her, he'd showed that he was a man of honour, she saw it every day.

In the way he treated his family, and the love he held for his niece and nephew, which was obvious to anyone who saw the three of them together, he demonstrated how much of an amazing father he would be.

As she lay there dreaming about what it would be like to be free enough to explore a future with this man; a saying that Charmaine had always said came to mind. On the nights that they sat outside discussing her family, and the torment that had been her childhood, her best friend would remind her that in life, there is hope, and that in love, there is freedom.

If only that were true.

Hope and freedom seemed like two foreign concepts at the moment.

Paris wanted nothing more than for them to be real, because right here, wrapped in Chance's arms, she had a feeling that she was already falling in love.

But that love would not bring her freedom, it would only bring herself and him pain.

Paris knew deep in the dark crevasses of her heart that there was no way she could allow her life the freedom she wanted until she could prove what happened that night in Seattle was not an accident.

She just hoped that when the truth did come out about the death of her friend and her past, Chance and Carly would be there for her, but she also knew in reality, the truth of the matter was that like everyone else they would probably turn their backs on her.

Yet even as she laid there pondering the 'what if's' and knowing that she had to stop this madness before she fell even harder, Paris could not bring herself to walk out of his arms and the comfort he provided.

"Hey, what's on your mind?" Chance drawled, squeezing her a little.

Paris hadn't realised that she had tensed.

Paris didn't know how in the world she was going to answer that. She wanted to tell him everything, share every wish she had for a future, but she also knew she couldn't very well tell him the truth.

This thing was only just new and even though he had made the first move, and considering his history with woman, Paris knew that if he found out the truth now, he would not stick around long enough to hear the whole truth. Considering that she came from a family who made their fortune coning people out of their money, she knew Chance would end this here and now and turn her out on her ear. He would see it as a ploy to gain what no other woman could.

Paris lay there silently running her fingers in circles around his chest, trying to think of a way to put her feelings into words without jeopardising what they had.

She must have been silent for too long, Chance squeezed

her once more, and with more worry in his tone than had been present before he repeated her name.

"Paris?" She knew he meant it as a question, but she could also hear the underlying concern there as well.

How was she ever going to give this man up?

Turning around in his arms, she leant up on her elbow, rested her chin in her palm and answered.

"I was just thinking about how amazing this night has been, and as much as I would like to do it again sometime."

Paris watched as a smile started to spread across his face, and he was just getting ready to kiss her again. He was wearing the same look he had last night when he had made himself known in the gazebo.

Paris sat up, grabbed her dress and pulled it across herself before she turned back to face him. He was lying flat on his back; his hands were behind his head and Paris was gifted with a view of his magnificent naked body. She groaned. This was going to be harder than she thought. Especially with his enticing body hers for the taking.

Chance rolled onto his side and started to run his free hand down her back, sending tingles spreading through her body wherever he went. Paris closed her eyes and tried to focus on what she was saying.

"There is no reason we can't keep this going while you are here. As you said, it was amazing, so why should we deny ourselves something that obviously so good for us." Chance replied as he leant forward and kissed the inside of one of her thighs.

Paris moaned. God how she wanted this man. But it was not fair to him, or her to continue this when she knew her feelings were getting too involved.

"No, we can't." Paris answered stopping him in his seduction of her.

Chance lay back on the makeshift bed once more, placed

his hands behind his head, narrowed his eyes on her and asked.

"Pray tell me why not."

She could see the doubt and suspicion enter his eyes; great this was all she needed. The last thing she wanted was for him to consider her in the same league as his last girl-friends.

"Don't even go there." She demanded before she continued. "I am worried what will happen if your sister finds out. I admire your sister and value our friendship, the last thing I want to do is jeopardise that. *And* on top of that, I love my job and I have no desire to lose that."

Paris had dropped her dress in her declaration and had turned to face him more fully. She was now as naked as he was, which was not the prime position to be in for a serious talk.

Chance rolled back onto his side, leaning onto his elbow once more placing his head in the palm of his hand. Leaning forward, he kissed her.

"Nobody has to know, if that is what you would like. I do know how to be discrete you know." He laughed.

Paris gave him a weak smile. She wanted to believe what he was saying, but she also needed the excuse to keep her distance. Paris knew that if he gave her a good enough argument to allay her logic, she would have no reason not to continue, and she would fall even harder.

"We don't have to stop this. We will just have to be careful is all. Please Paris, tell me you don't want to stop this."

Paris took a deep breath and thought about it.

She was not kidding anyone but herself. She wanted to keep this going as much as he did. The question was not if she wanted to keep this going, it was did she have the strength to walk away when the end came.

And the answer to that was no. She knew without a doubt

that if she kept this thing going it was only going to make it harder on herself when she left, and she *would* leave.

She had to.

Chance moved a piece of stray hair back behind her ear as he watched her contemplate what he had offered.

As his eyes watched her Paris knew it would not take much more for her to lose herself to him. Her heart was already engaged, way too much, she had to make sure her head stayed strong. She was just about to argue his last point with him when he gave her another option.

"Look, let's not make any rash decisions tonight. Let's give it a few weeks and see how we go."

Paris opened her mouth to add something, but he placed his hand on her mouth.

"I was not finished. If at any time in the next few weeks any of this becomes too much for you, we will revisit it then. But for now, let's just have some fun."

While her heart was screaming at her to say yes, and brain was screaming no, Paris could only laugh at the eager look in his eyes. The longer they sat there staring at each other the quieter the voice in her head became and the louder her heart sounded.

She could use a bit of fun in her life at the moment.

And realistically, what harm could a few more weeks do? She was already practically in love with him, a few weeks would not make that much of a difference, or so she thought.

"Okay, but if it gets too complicated, we call it quits with no bad feelings. Deal?" Paris stuck out her hand, waiting for him to agree to her terms. It took him a minute, but then a sly smile spread across his face.

"Damn woman, you are like a dream come true. Deal," he said, reaching out and shaking her hand. Paris laughed when he grabbed her and rolled her on top of him.

"Now let's start this affair the right way." He smiled, placing his hand on her arse, anchoring her to himself.

"And how would that be?" Paris teased, kissing the hollow in his throat. She planned to drive him as wild has he'd driven her last night, and a smile of satisfaction spread across her face, when her tongue dipping into that hollow elicited a groan of pleasure from him.

But the teasing soon stopped when he entered her in one swift movement.

"Oh, I like this much better," she hissed as he started to move.

Soon all thoughts but what was happening left Paris and as she neared her peak, she prayed that for a small time she could enjoy the happiness she had found here.

Because she knew that sooner or later her world would come crashing down around her, then her freedom and her happiness would end.

What Paris was unaware of was that day was going to come sooner rather than later, and it was going to come in a form she would never suspect.

CHAPTER SIXTEEN

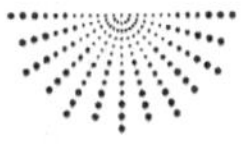

Liz pulled up to the front of the ranch, switched off her car and looked in the mirror to make sure her makeup was perfect.

While things weren't going as planned, she knew that all she had to do was get Chance to remember why they were good for each other and she would be back on the road to gaining what she wanted.

And what she wanted was this ranch, the man who came with it was an added bonus.

Liz knew from the moment her father moved them here that she no longer wanted to be the daughter of a cattle salesmen, running around sales yards, moving from town to town, never knowing what it felt like to have the riches that the ranches did.

That was until she ended up in Cody.

She still remembered the day she first learned about Chance. It was about a year ago, when he had brought his herd to the cattle yards. Liz had just had another fight with her father about her spending, and she decided then and there that she was going to go on the hunt for a sugar daddy so to speak.

Then in walked Chance.

She was so happy, not only was she going to get the money she wanted, but she wasn't going to have to marry some old smelly rancher.

Her plan had been working, the next few months she spent her time running into Chance in town and when they finally did hook up it had been amazing.

Although Liz never loved Chance and would never love him, she only loved his money, the sex was to die for. He was a God in bed, had money and was as sexy as hell; Liz knew she was never going to let him go. She was determined to get Chance to marry her no matter what it took.

Everything had been on track, but when Liz had brought up marriage Chance had pulled away, and that was how they ended up here.

Liz was not upset about the loss of the romance; she was pissed about losing her opportunity at gaining this ranch. And now his meddling sister was here trying to find a way out of the mess her brother had created.

But Liz had news for Carly, there was only one way out and that was marriage.

For now though, she was happy to go along with their pathetic attempts to get her to back down, but in the end they would learn, marriage was what she wanted and that was what she would get.

Liz smiled a wicked smile into the mirror, fixed a stray hair.

"Let's get the show on the road." She whispered, before placing on her sweet face.

She was a woman of many roles, and the one she needed to play now was the sweet, hurt, jilted lover. She had to make everyone feel sorry for her, thus turning on Chance. She needed everyone to think of him as the monster in this scenario.

So far it wasn't working. Most of the town and his workers were taking his side, but she knew if she kept on trying it would work, eventually.

Opening the door, Liz stepped out of her car and made her way to the house.

She was just rounding the corner that would lead to the front when the door flew open and Carly's brats flew out the door and down the stairs, they were shouting at one another, but then they stopped and shouted back at the house.

"Paris hurry up, we want to get to the river." With that they were rushing off again.

"Don't go too far ahead." Liz heard yelled from the front door.

"Okay," they both cried in unison. Liz was going to make herself known but decided to give it a few more minutes.

She was glad she did.

Liz watched on as a beautiful woman walked out the door and onto the veranda.

She was in the process of putting on her shoes, that was nothing out of the ordinary, but what happened next had Liz's blood boiling.

It took everything in her control not to rip this woman's eyes out. Before Liz could make herself known, Chance stepped out of the house, placing his hat on his head.

Liz expected him to simply greet the girl and keep on walking, but he didn't, instead he slapped her arse, before leaving his hand there to rub her derriere. In all their time together, Chance had never been that carefree with her.

The girl straightened and punched him in the chest.

"Chance cut it out. Low profile, remember."

"Relax Hunny, there is no-one around. Plus, don't you

know it is every man's fantasy to be able to say they are sleeping with the nanny."

The girl punched him again.

"Alright I concede." He said holding his hands up, walking slowly down the stairs. But once he was at the bottom the look he gave her was one filled with so much heat, Liz could feel it from where she was standing. She had to grab hold of the porch pillars to keep herself from moving.

"Fine, but later on tonight I plan to show you just what you do to me woman."

The girl leaned up against the porch and licked her lips before giving him a smile that would light up the world.

"Oh, I am counting on it." Chance winked at her before he headed off towards the bunkhouse. The girl watched him go before she herself headed off after the children. It took a few more moments for Liz to gather her wits back, but once she had a new fire settled in.

Who the hell did this girl think she was, how dare she come in here and think she could steal everything Liz had worked so hard to gain?

She had to make a plan.

Liz paced for a few minutes before a plan started to form. The only way she was going to get this girl out of the picture was to make her leave. With that in mind, Liz headed into her meeting with Carly. This meeting was going to serve a new purpose, while Carly tried her hardest to get Liz to drop her vendetta and come up with a solution that would make them all happy, Liz only had one thing on her mind; gaining as much information as she could about the nanny.

This girl was going to be sorry she ever met Chance.

Liz was pissed.

The only information she had been able to garner from Chance's know-it-all meddling sister was that the nanny was a teacher, from Seattle. The moment Liz had tried to get any more information she had cut the conversation short and went into business mode.

Liz slammed the door of her car and headed into her modest, cheap house which was attached to the cattle yards. She shared the house with her father, as she could not afford a place on her own.

As she walked past the yards to the front door the usual smells of cow shit and dirty animals assailed her nose. This coupled with the morning she had, saw Liz slamming her way into the house, cursing.

"God damn stupid bitch." She fired. "There is no way she is going to take what is mine." She continued to rant, as she stormed through the house to her room.

"Liz is that you?" Her father called to her, just as she opened the computer.

"Of course it's me, who the hell else would it be." She mumbled under her breath. Liz wanted to scream and yell at him, but she couldn't. She needed her father on her side.

He was after all the one that was helping her screw up Chance's life. He of course thought he was saving his daughter from a lying scum of a rancher, when in truth he had no idea that is was her who was lying.

When Chance had broken up with her, she had become distraught over the loss of her way out of this hell. All her father however had seen was his broken-hearted princess. She ran with the lie, convincing her father that Chance had promised to marry her, but had changed his mind, once he got what he had wanted. Her father of course had sworn that he would ruin Chance, unless he kept his promise.

And that was exactly what he was doing. So, for now Liz

had to keep a calm head around her father. If he ever found out the truth, he would send her to live with her mother in the trailer park where she resided, where she would have to work in the local dive, right alongside her.

There was nothing wrong with the life her mother chose to live, she was happy, and that was the main thing.

But it was not the life Liz wanted.

No. Liz wanted money. She wanted status and she wanted luxury. The only way she was going to get that was with Chance.

"Yeah it's me, Dad." She replied as calmly as she could.

She hoped that her father would leave her be, and she as just about to get the privacy she wanted.

Before long, her father's head poked around her door.

"I'm just heading into town for a few supplies. Do you need anything?" he asked.

Liz smiled at him.

Know a good hit man?

"No, I am fine thanks."

"Okay I will see you in a few."

Liz waited a few more moments until the sound of her father's footsteps had faded, and the sound of his car replaced them.

Once she was sure she was alone, Liz started doing her own research. She started by googling Paris to see if anything that would come up, but without her last name it was useless.

She then tried Paris and Seattle. Again, it lowered the search, but it was still too broad.

Using the last bit of information, she had, Liz searched once more for teachers named Paris in Seattle. At first, she thought she was going to hit another dead end, but on the fourth page of the search Liz fell upon an interesting video.

Opening the video, she watched in fascination as a

brother pleaded with anyone who knew the whereabouts of his missing sister to get in contact with him.

It was Paris. She knew it.

Those without a discerning eye would have missed it as the girl in the photo was blonde, whereas the Paris she had seen today was a brunette. On top of that the girl in the picture was few years younger, but when one really looked at the picture, the features of the girl at the ranch started to come through.

Yes, this was the break she needed.

Liz wanted her gone, and what better way to do that than to have her family come and collect her.

With an evil smile planted on her face, Liz picked up the phone and dialled the number on the screen.

It didn't take long before a voice came through the other end.

"Hello."

Liz took a breath before she spoke. "Hello, is this Tommy Michaels?"

"This is he." The way in which he was answering gave Liz the feeling that he was not in the mood for games. Well neither was she. The sooner she got this over with the better.

"I know where your sister is." She added before he could say anymore.

Liz had expected the man on the other end to be joyous and beg her to tell him where she was. Instead there was a moment pause and then hushed voices as though he was speaking to someone else.

"Hello." Liz said trying to gain his attention.

"Are you sure it is her?" The voice asked. There was no joy, only irritation and urgency.

She was kind of pissed that this man even dared to question her, so her tone was a bit snappy when she replied.

"Of course, I'm sure, now do you want to know where she is or not?"

She had expected the man to be angry, so Liz was taken back when he laughed a bitter laugh.

"Well by all means tell us."

Liz briefly wondered if she was doing the right thing. She wanted Chance; that was a no brainer, but was she willing to put an innocent girl in the hands of the cold man on the other end of the phone.

Flashes of Chance's hands on the girl's arse flashed in her mind along with another whiff of cow shit, and she knew she would do anything. The girl's life meant nothing to her, only her own life and happiness mattered.

"Your sister is in Cody, Wyoming, at a ranch called Blackridge."

"You will be rewarded handsomely if it turns out you are correct. I just need your name and number Love."

Liz's skin crawled with the way he said that, there was no way she wanted anything from this man.

"You collecting your sister is the only reward I need, so hurry up and get here."

She didn't wait around to see if there was any reply. She simply hung up. Now all she had to do was wait.

Wait to see if her plan worked. Then her life could get back to normal.

CHAPTER SEVENTEEN

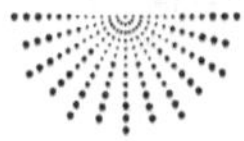

Paris couldn't believe that it had been last week Chance and she had started their little affair, and she had never been happier. All of the doubts she'd had about it at first had washed away within days.

True to his word, Chance had kept their relationship a secret. When people were around, he acted as though they were nothing more than friends, but when they were alone, *that* was a completely different story.

Paris smiled to herself as she thought back over the last week. When she had first arrived, she never would have suspected that underneath the rough, rude cowboy that greeted her outside the bathroom, would be a gentle kind-hearted man. A man she wished she could spend every day with for the rest of her life.

In the last week, Chance surprised her at every turn, he took every opening he could to sneak in kisses and caresses, and at night when they were alone, he spoilt her with moonlight picnics and swims, or horseback rides across the countryside. In the last few weeks, Paris had been shown the entire ranch, and she had loved every moment of it.

Paris had an inkling that Carly knew something was going on. It wasn't so much was she did, it was more what she had said one night while they were having their nightly drink.

"Chance seems a lot happier these days." She had commented. The comment itself was nothing unusual. But the way Carly was looking over her glass at Paris said volumes.

"Hadn't noticed." Paris said offhandedly.

She dared a look at Carly who was looking at her with a knowing sort of look. Thankfully she didn't say anything other than,

"Mmm. Well he is. It's nice to see."

Paris smiled into her glass, knowing that she was the reason for it.

"I'm sure it is." she offered as a reply.

Paris had to agree with Carly. Chance was definitely happier, as was she. But that was also becoming part of a bigger problem.

The longer she stayed, the harder it was becoming to leave.

But she had to leave. There was no way around that knowledge, and while Paris spent most of her nights trying to figure out a way for her to stay, she also knew that if she did, she would have to come clean about what happened in Seattle, and she wasn't sure she could do that.

Paris had spent the morning with the children riding the ranch. They wanted to show her the places they loved. And while she had seen most of it with Chance at night, during the day it was so different and she couldn't deny them. That had been the morning activities.

It did however lead them to the lesson they had just finished. While on the ride Nerada had asked Paris to explain the difference between a horse and a donkey. And that lead to them talking about the different groups of animals.

Heading back to the barn, the next few hours were spent exploring the different animals on the farm and what made them what they were.

That had taken them two hours. Now it was time for lunch.

Walking out of the barn, Paris headed around to the outside sink and turned on the water. She was just washing up so that she could head inside and enjoy lunch. She smiled when she heard the kids yelling out to her. "Paris, we have finished, now what do you want us to do?"

"Well, first of all, I want you to come here and wash your hands, then, I want you to head up into the house and have lunch. We have a big afternoon of gardening to do." Paris laughed as they both whooped and hollered, splashing water everywhere.

Both Paris and Carly had been surprised at how much the children had loved the idea of starting their own garden. It had come to her one day over lunch when the kids had asked their mother where the fruit they ate came from.

Paris decided that not only would it teach the kids about self-reliance, it would also give her the chance teach them some more Maths, Science and a bit of Industrial Design Technology. Paris knew that Carly was ecstatic with how her children's education was coming along, after all Carly had thanked her enough over the last few weeks. She had even made a comment that the children had learnt more in their time with her than they had all year. Paris had to admit that it was not all he doing, it helped that they had a one on one education with a teacher.

Paris continued to watch the children as they ran towards the house. They were halfway there when they stopped and turned towards her.

"Are you coming?" they yelled.

"I will be there in a minute," she yelled back as Paris realised that she had forgotten her hat in the barn, normally she would have left it there, but she would need it for later and she knew the kids would want to get straight to it. Lunch could wait a few more minutes.

Paris walked back inside the cool barn it was nice being in here away from the heat of the Wyoming sun.

If she wasn't so hungry, she would have stopped a while longer to greet the horses, but her stomach was screaming at her. Riding the range and examining animals sure worked up an appetite.

Grabbing her hat, Paris made her way back towards the entrance of the barn. She had almost made it when someone grabbed her from behind.

Letting out a scream, Paris turned in the arms of her captor and was about to fight for her freedom, when the laughing eyes of Chance met hers.

"You jerk, you frightened me." She said, slapping at his arms.

She wanted to stay mad at him, but the cheeky smile that he was giving her, and the sparkle in his eyes had her melting like jelly.

"I'm sorry, but I couldn't pass up the chance to hold you in my arms." He whispered as he backed her up against the wall and captured her mouth with his. The kiss that he gave her was filled with the same longing she had for him. Every day that passed it was getting harder for her not to show her affection for him. She loved being in his strong arms, and when he passed her in kitchen in the mornings, she wanted nothing more than for him to kiss her as he was now. With each brush of his arm, or whiff of his cologne, her resolve to keep their relationship on a friendship level in the presence of others was becoming almost impossible.

The little moments that they captured like this were not enough.

She wanted him all the time.

But she had to keep in mind the end result. It would be disastrous if someone found out. Especially the wrong person.

With that in mind Paris tried to bring some reason to what was happening.

"Chance, someone could come..." He didn't give her a chance to finish. He simply captured her mouth once more and deepened the kiss.

Paris knew she should protest some more, but the feelings that were building up inside of her, the feelings he always evoked were overriding any line of reasoning she had.

All she could think about was what was happening.

As he showered love on her mouth, his hand made its way underneath her dress, until his fingers moved her panties aside and entered her core.

Paris sucked in a depth breath and let out a moan that filled the barn.

"Are you *sure* you want me to stop?" he asked as he trailed his mouth down her neck to the top of her dress.

Paris wanted to answer him, she knew she should stop him before this went much further, but she could not form a coherent thought.

"No answer, I guess that means you want me to continue."

Paris moaned once more as he moved lower and the sensation of his teeth around her nipple through her dress drove her beyond the point of no return.

She knew it was wrong

She knew she should stop it.

And yet, she did not have the will power to do so.

Paris let the feelings he was causing rush through her for

a moment more. Just once more couldn't hurt could it, she thought as he moved his way over to her other breast.

This time however he was not happy with tasting her through her dress, he wanted flesh. The moment the cool summer air in the barn touched her chest, Paris was brought to her sense.

"Chance," she said again, this time with more force. She placed her hands on his shoulder effectively stopping his movements.

He did pause in his administrations, and for a brief moment Paris prayed that he would do the right thing and walk away. She needed him to be the stronger person, because there was no way she could walk away.

"So, what you are telling me right now, is that you want this…" he punctuated his words by moving the two fingers he still had inside of her, "to stop."

Paris couldn't answer him if she tried, he had only moved his fingers once, but it had been enough to push her close to the edge. She was just about to answer him when he moved them again, which caused her to shake her head no.

Chance gave her a knowing grin. With that grin came the knowledge that this man could break her heart. That thought was like an ice-cold bath raining down on her, her thoughts started to clear, and she nodded instead.

Chance's eyes narrowed.

"Really?" he asked, accentuating his words with his fingers once more. But this time he not only moved the two that were inside of her, he added his thumb and circled her clit, causing small shudders to rip through her body.

She was so close to losing it; she needed him to see reason before she could no longer find the words.

Paris' head fell back against the barn wall, her hand grabbed hold of the wrist that was under and dress and held it tight to stop him from moving it anymore. She needed to make him see sense, and in order for her to do that she needed to make sure her mind was clear.

When his hand didn't move again, she tried once more to convince him.

"Chance be reasonable. Someone could come in here and find us. God it could even be the kids. They know I am in here." The only answer she got was his fingers moving once more.

"Chance, PLEASE." She pleaded.

As the words left her mouth Paris wasn't sure if she was pleading with him to continue or stop.

But she didn't have time to think about it anymore, because with his next words and actions all thoughts of stopping left her completely.

"Well I will just have to take your mind off that worry, won't I," he answered, right before he knelt in front of her.

Seeing him kneeling in front of her, his eyes boring into hers was the most erotic thing she had ever seen. She didn't think she would ever be able to erase the image from her mind.

She knew she was meant to be stopping him, instead all she could do was watch as he lifted her dress and replaced his fingers with his mouth.

The moan that left her came from somewhere deep within. Grabbing his head, she held him there as he sucked her clit and tongued her core like a master.

He sucked and tongued her until she was teetering on the edge of the most amazing orgasm she was ever going to have, just a few more strokes she thought and she would be riding in the stars.

A small whimper left her mouth when he stopped and looked up at her. The glint in his eyes should have told her that he was up to something, but she still was not suspecting the words that followed.

"Do you still want me to stop? I am after all a gentleman and I would hate to make you do something you don't want to." he asked with a cheeky grin on his face.

He was giving her one last opportunity to change her mind. The ball was now in her court.

How did he keep on doing this to me?

"If you do, you will be sorry." Paris panted.

Chance let out a boom of laughter right before he placed his mouth back on her core.

The reverberations of his laughter, coupled with his masterful tongue, had Paris coming within seconds of his new onslaught.

Chance lapped at her a few more times before he rose before her, giving her a quick kiss. Paris could not move; she couldn't even quite open her eyes yet. That had so been worth the risk of getting caught.

Paris slowly opened her eyes and was greeted by his gorgeous face. He was in no rush to move and neither was she. Chance ran his fingers over her cheek and placed a piece of hair that had escaped back behind her ears. A small smile played on her lips at the tenderness he was showing, it must have triggered something in him as the next moment he was leaning forward, pinning her to the wall once more.

She loved how he couldn't stop kissing her, she didn't mind in the least.

She loved how he tasted, of lemon and lime. It was uniquely him.

But most of all she loved all of him.

As he once again deepened the kiss, Paris closed her eyes and soaked up every feeling she felt for him. She didn't want this moment to stop, and she almost cried when he pulled away from her.

She wanted to pull him close to her again, but the bulge

that was pressing against his trousers told her that was probably not a good idea.

"There, that should hold me until later," he whispered into her ear, sending shivers over her skin from where his breath landed. Paris leaned her head to the side a little which allowed him to trail kisses along her jaw.

When he was finished, he stood legs apart so that he was the same height as her, while his hands rested on the wall just above her head. Paris stared at him through lust-filled eyes.

"That was…" She tried to articulate exactly what she was feeling, but she couldn't get her words to work.

"I know." He simply said, winking.

"Now you had better get back to the house and have some lunch before someone comes looking for you."

Paris looked out the window of the barn that was behind him, she could see that the sun was making its path high in the sky. She was not sure how long they had been here like this, but she was sure that any minute now the children would come searching for her. It did not take a person that long to find a hat.

Paris could only nod before she straightened her dress and turned to walk out.

Chance slapped her butt playfully as she passed him, she turned around and offered him a smile.

"I look forward to repaying the favour later." She offered him sassily.

She was pleased to see that her comment wiped the cocky smile off his face. Instead the look of laughter he'd worn moments before was replaced with pure lust. She could see it in his eyes, and in the way he was standing.

"You had better leave now before I take you up on that offer." His husky voiced reached her.

Paris took a moment to get moving, she contemplated if they could get away with it, but another look towards the house saw that fantasy crash and burn. It was only a matter of minutes before someone came looking, she was sure of it.

Instead, Paris simply gave him a cocksure smile before she sauntered out of the barn. She had made it halfway across the yard when she realised that she had still forgotten her hat, she wondered if she could go back it get it. But when she turned and looked back, it was to see Chance leaning against the barn door, his eyes hooded and full of lust; nope the hat would have to wait.

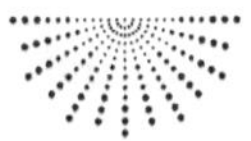

CHAPTER EIGHTEEN

Turning back toward the house, trying to put Chance out of her mind, Paris continued her journey up to the porch.

Thankfully she here the kids were still engaged in telling their mother all about their morning.

Paris took a moment to calm her nerves and make sure she was put together. Reaching up she smoothed down her hair and then made sure her dress was in its proper place.

Content that everything was where it was supposed to be, Paris reached for the door when a voice off to the side caught her attention.

"You know he is only using you, don't you?"

Paris gave a little squeak, and with her hand on her heart she turned to where the voice was coming from.

Paris' heart leapt into her throat when she saw Liz leaning against the railing.

Paris quickly looked back to the barn and let out a sigh of relief to see that Chance was no longer standing there. But as she looked back at Liz, Paris had a feeling that it wouldn't have mattered anyway, her instincts told her that this woman knew what had just transpired between her and Chance, and if the look on her face was any indication, she was not happy about it.

There was only one thing Paris could do, fake it. She had been doing it for so long now, Paris felt as though it had become part of her personality. Pasting a look of confusion on her face, along with a friendly smile, Paris looked Liz square in the eyes.

"I have no idea what you are talking about." She said hoping that the woman would buy her lie and just drop it.

But as luck would have it, she didn't. Instead Liz pushed herself away from the railing and walked slowly towards Paris, speaking as she did.

"Oh yes you do. I *know* that look you wear. And I saw him watching you as you left the barn. You two think you have been so smart in hiding, whatever this is. But I am her to tell you right now that you can't have him. He is mine and you should know that no matter how much you screw him, he *will* remember that."

Paris should have been shocked by what this woman was saying, but she wasn't.

The thing that Liz didn't know was that Paris was used to vipers such as Liz. After all, when you grow up in a house full of them, one tends to grow accustomed to their bite.

Yes Liz probably thought she had the upper hand, and she probably even thought she could scare Paris off with her weak-arse threat, but what Liz didn't know is that in order for her lame plan to work, Paris had to play into her ploy, and that she wouldn't do.

Paris wasn't going to let this woman know that she was correct, but she wasn't going to let her lies continue either. Letting go of the door Paris leaned her shoulder against the wall.

She kept her voice low as she answered.

"Well, as for whatever you think is going on with me and Chance, that is your own delusion and there is nothing I can do about that. But from what I hear, you are the only one that thinks he belongs with you. And quite frankly, speaking from a woman's perspective, it's pathetic how you continue to chase him when everyone, even your father, knows that he wants nothing to do with you. Why don't you do yourself a favour and leave his family alone before everyone, including, this town and your own family, realises how pathetic and crazy you are?"

Paris felt good to get that out, she felt like she had won some unknown battle. That was until she saw the fire build in the crazy woman's eyes.

What had she been thinking? Getting into a bitch fight with a crazy woman was *not* keeping a low profile. She should have just ignored the viper's comments and left things alone. Chance's troubles were not her fight to fight.

Paris stood up straight when Liz stared marching towards her, fists balled tight at her side. She started backing up until her but was against the railing. Not out of fear, but out of self-preservation. The last thing Paris needed was to get into a brawl that would see the police involved.

But Paris had no-where else to go and Liz was practically standing on Paris toes.

Paris was considering what her best move was, when the next words out of Liz's mouth paralysed her.

"Oh, you think you are so smart don't you, bitch, but I have news for you. You are not as smart as you think you are, and you and I both know you are not as innocent as you make out to be, oh no you are not."

Paris did not like where this was going at all, and as much as she wanted to run, her feet were glued to the porch as the woman moved even closer, they were now nose-to-nose.

Paris could see the crazy in her eyes. Her heart raced, and her palms began to sweat.

It was not so much the words that had left Liz's mouth that caused the terror to run rampant in her blood, it was more the way she said it.

The fear that someone would find out had been with her for months. And that fear was now in overdrive thinking that someone had finally found out her secret.

And not just anyone, the one person who had nothing to lose with her being gone.

How could you have been so stupid to let down your guard? Her mind screamed at her.

When Liz next spoke, the words came out in a whisper. "I know *exactly* who you are, Miss *Michaels*, and I know *exactly* why you are here.

Paris' heart pounded so violently; she was worried that she was about to have a heart attack. It was not so much that she had admitted to knowing about the murder, it was more the use of her family name that sent chills up her spine.

Paris took a deep breath she needed to calm down and think this through. If this woman was telling the truth, the real truth that she knew why Paris was here, wouldn't the police already be here?

The real question that bugged Paris was the one of how Liz knew her real name.

"What exactly do you think you know?" Paris asked calmly once more.

She manoeuvred her way around Liz and started to make her way back towards the door.

"Well I know that you are on the run from your family and that they are looking for you. I also know that they should be here any day now. I also know that once you are out of the picture, I will be able to get Chance to notice me again."

Well Paris was thankful that at least she hadn't mentioned the murder, but that would have been a better scenario than the one she was facing now.

Could she really have called her family?

Was her father dumb enough to risk exposure to come and collect her himself?

Paris didn't have answers for any of these questions, and the only way she would know the truth was to turn that damn television on. But Paris knew that if she did that would risk opening a whole new tin of worms.

Right now, the only thing Paris needed to do was get away from this woman.

She needed time and space to think.

One thing Paris was thankful for was her ability to appear calm in any situation. While her internal state was slowly melting down, her outside exterior appeared as though the two of them were having nothing more than a wonderful afternoon chat. That allowed Paris to answer with more calm than she felt.

"Oh, I am sorry you went to all that trouble, but my name is Tailor and my family already know where I am. In fact, I spoke to my mother just last night and they are actually planning a weekend trip up here soon."

Paris felt a little twinge of happiness to see the rage cross over her face once more.

"Now if you wouldn't mind, I have some lunch to eat and planning to do."

Paris walked back to the door and was just about to open it when Liz's words hit her ears.

"Keep pretending bitch, I guess we will find out the truth in the next few days. I just might give your *brother* another call to see how far away they are."

Paris' heart was thumping in her chest so hard that it was starting to hurt. Paris was finding it hard to take in deep breaths. She needed to get away from this woman as fast as possible, so without saying another word, Paris opened the door and entered the hallway, the woman's evil laughter following her.

CHAPTER NINETEEN

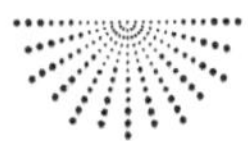

Paris was not sure how she had figured it out, but she was certain that Liz knew exactly who she was. There was only one way for her to find out for sure, Paris hid just inside the doorway and watched Liz retreat off the porch, her phone in hand, dialling a number.

Leaning forward, Paris tried to hear what the phone call was about.

"Yes, hello Tommy, I was just wanting to..." Liz's words were cut short as she got into her car. Paris' panic started to rise, now that she was alone a full-blown panic attack was starting to hit her. Looking around the room, she tried to get her mind to slow down when voices from the kitchen drew her there.

Paris had to calm herself. Just because she was talking to someone named Tommy, did not mean that it was indeed Paris' brother. The name was quite popular over here after all. Talking a calming breath and trying to calm her speeding heart, Paris made her way to the kitchen.

When she entered, the kids were still eating and talking

to their mother. A sad smile twitched across Paris' face at the thought of leaving. She knew it would have happened eventually, but the reality of the matter was, she had secretly hoped it would never come.

It was only in that moment that Paris realised how much she loved them all, including Chance.

The realisation of that love brought with it the one that there was no way she could bring all of her trouble down on their heads.

She owed to them to leave and take her problems with her. Paris considered proving Liz wrong so that she could stay, but she also knew that it would not work. Liz was out for blood and if she didn't get Paris to leave this time, she would eventually find the truth, and in doing so Paris would lose the love and respect of all those she held dear here.

Leaving was her only option.

"Is something wrong?" Carly asked Paris, her face filled with concern.

Paris hadn't realised that she had been standing in the doorway staring at the trio as they ate lunch. She wanted desperately to lie to Carly once more and say no. She wanted desperately for it to be the truth.

But it wasn't.

Instead, Paris just added another lie to the ones she had been telling for months.

"I'm just not feeling well that's all. I think I might go up to bed and retire for a bit."

At the kids' disappointed moans, Paris gave them a sad smile. She knelt down near the table and ruffled Leo's hair.

"It's just for a little while, and if I don't feel better today, I promise we will work in the garden first thing tomorrow."

Both kids, nodded solemnly before they went back to eating their lunch. Her heart hurt knowing the she was letting them down, but she knew it was going to hurt even more tomorrow knowing they would wake up to her being gone, breaking her promise and not knowing why.

Tears were threating to spill, luckily Carly stepped in.

"Don't worry about that, we would rather you feel better, that way you can do more fun things other days. Right kids?"

Their apologetic eyes showed that they hadn't thought about that. Both of them jumped out of their chairs and ran up to hug her around her waist.

"Of course, we would rather you feel better."

"Do you want us to read you a book?" Nerada asked innocently.

"I would love that, I really would. But for now, I think I just need some sleep."

Paris had to get out of here soon or she was going to crack.

The children hugged for a moment longer, before they went back to eating lunch.

Paris took the out they had given her and headed from the kitchen into the living room. She had just reached the door when Carly's voice reached her.

"Don't worry about coming back down tonight, I will send you up some dinner. You rest."

Paris walked back into the kitchen and hugged Carly. No-one, besides Charmaine had cared for her the way Carly did. She had become the sister she had always wanted, and this was probably going to be the last time Paris ever saw her.

Paris let Carly go and headed for her room once more. Paris planned to head straight to her room, but when she entered the lounge room the television caught her eye.

This was her opportunity to see if Liz had been telling the truth. Maybe by some miracle, Paris could get a few more weeks here before she had to leave.

Checking the kitchen, she was happy to see that the family was still preoccupied with their lunch stories.

Taking a calming breath, Paris walked towards the TV, she picked up the remote, turned it on and turned the volume right down.

She wanted to check to see if Liz had been telling the truth.

Was her family really appealing to the public to help find her, was there any truth to what Liz had been implying. Could her family right this minute be on their way to Blackridge Ranch?

Flipping through the channels, Paris' breath hitched when she hit the news, and there was exactly what she had been dreading from the moment she left Seattle.

Seattle Police are still looking for any witnesses in the brutal killing of Charmaine Cole at the Hyatt Hotel in June. They are also asking the public to come forward with any information they might have pertaining to the whereabouts of one Miss Paris Devon, Miss Cole's roommate. If you have any....

Paris couldn't watch any more of that, she kind of had a feeling that the police would be looking for her. At least they still hadn't claimed her as a suspect. It still didn't answer her question as to whether Liz was right.

Then Paris landed on a channel that made all of her nightmares come true. Standing there in front of the camera appealing to the public to help find his sister's whereabouts was one of the men from the night at the hotel. But that was not what caught her attention. The phot of herself up in the corner, along with the man standing off to the right held her transfixed.

The photo was of her, just before she came to the States and the man standing off to the right of her supposed brother, was her father.

Liz had been telling the truth, and her father was right now on his way here to get her.

"Whatcha watching?" Chance drawled from the doorway of the kitchen.

Paris squeaked and quickly turned the TV off and turned to him. She had been so terrified, knowing that her father was on his way here that she hadn't even heard anyone enter the room.

Paris knew that she had to look guilty with the speed she had turned off the TV, and with her strange reaction to his appearance but she couldn't help it. All she could do now was muddle through.

Planting a smile on her face, she leaned her hip against the couch and replied.

"Nothing, I was seeing if there was anything good to curl up in front of. But it turns out I would rather be in bed. I am not feeling too well."

Chance narrowed his eyes at her, he was still leaning against the door frame, his cowboy boots crossed over each other, while his muscular arms matched, crossed over his chest.

He was still wearing his hat.

As he stood there staring at her, the fire from earlier was still in his eyes. Memories of the barn washed over her, and she prayed that he hadn't seen anything on the TV. She wanted him to remember her the way they had been this afternoon.

"Is there anything I can do to help you feel better, Sugar?" he threw in as he pushed away from the door and headed towards her.

As Paris watched him saunter over to her, she was again torn by the realisation that she was going to have to leave him. Never in a million years would she have thought that she would find the man she wanted to spend the rest of her life with. A man that was so far removed from the men in her family.

There was no way she could stay now, not with what Liz had discovered, her phone call, and with what Paris had seen on the news only confirmed her need to keep those she loved safe. And if she had to leave the only person she would ever love and wanted to keep him safe; then that was what she would do.

And if Paris was being honest with herself, leaving also meant that she would never have to see the heartache and feeling of betrayal that was sure to cross both his and Carly's faces when they found out the truth about her.

Leaving was her only option.

Wrapping herself into his embrace, she breathed in his smell – leather and horse, lemons and limes – one more time before answering.

"That is really sweet, but all I really need is some rest. I will have to give tonight a miss, but hopefully we can do a raincheck.

The sigh of disappointment that reverberated through is body was one that she herself felt. She could just have him for one more night, but Paris knew that wouldn't be fair to either of them, plus she needed to plan.

Deep down thought Paris hoped that he would try and persuade her, but being the gentleman that he was, Chance simply held her tighter.

"Of course we can, Sugar." He whispered as he kissed the top of her head.

He was doing it again, making her feel safe.

In his arms it felt like nothing in the world could touch her, but Paris knew that wasn't true.

It was time for her to let him go.

He deserved better than what she could give him.

Paris broke free of his hold, walking out of his embrace,

she gave him one last smile before she headed up to her room where she would decide what to do.

Who was she kidding, Paris knew there was only one thing she could do.

She was going to do what she had done all her life; she was going to run.

CHAPTER TWENTY

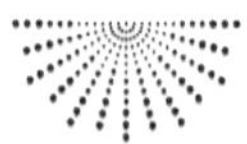

Chance watched Paris as she walked up the stairs and out of site, and as she did a feeling of dread entered his soul.

He could not put his finger on it, but he knew that while Paris had said she was feeling ill, Chance knew the truth.

She was pulling away from him.

After their little rendezvous in the barn that afternoon, Chance had left Paris feeling lighter than he ever had. He could still feel the feelings he had felt watching her walk up the stairs.

He had planned on watching her until she had entered the house, but Bronx had called him, needing his help with something.

Giving her one last look, Chance had headed back into the barn. On his way through he noticed Paris had left her hat behind. He smiled to himself because he now had a reason to look for her after he'd finished.

That had been the plan.

His plan came to a crashing halt, ten minutes later when he caught the tail end of Liz leaving. Watching her walk down the drive to her car, with a smug smile on her face turned his stomach.

He didn't have to be told that the meeting hadn't been pleasant, Paris stance as she stood by the door told him she was upset.

He should have been there to stop the confrontation. All he could do now was hope that Paris didn't believe a word she said.

Chance was just leaving the barn, getting ready to stop Paris and find out what the bitch had said to her, but Bronx had called him out to him once more.

Standing just outside the barn door, Chance watched as Paris entered the house, he was torn he wanted to go and sooth Paris, but Bronx's second call for help, told him he needed to attend to his chores first.

It took him only five minutes to help Bronx get a temperamental stallion back into his own yard, once that had been accomplished Chance hightailed it back to the house.

He had hoped to find Paris still at lunch with his sister. That would have let him know that everything was fine. But he found her sitting in the lounge room watching TV.

There was nothing unusual in the activity itself, it was more how she looked. Standing there watching whatever was on the screen, Paris looked a small lost girl. He had never seen her as anything but confident and sure of herself.

It broke his heart to think that a stupid decision on his part to hook up with the wrong woman was about to cost him the right one.

He just hoped that whatever damage Liz had done he could fix it. There was only one way he was going to find out.

Chance leaned against the door frame hoping to appear as though he was casual. He then cleared his throat.

"Whatcha watching?" he asked as casually as he could.

Although he looked calm and collected on the outside, there was a panic like he had never felt before rushing though his veins.

Chance was not ready to admit that he loved her, but he did know that he was not ready to lose her.

Paris was startled by his appearance, and she had turned the TV of quickly. Chance thought nothing of the action and simply put it down to her being startled.

That had been the last thing Chance had wanted to do, he had simply hoped to find out what was going on inside of her head.

While he waited for her to answer, all the memories from that afternoon came rushing forward and he couldn't wait to get her alone.

But now here he stood watching her walk up the stairs trying to figure out her strange reaction to his appearance. Now that he had put some distance between them her behaviour made him nervous.

It wasn't just that he had surprised her. No, she had seemed skittish.

What the hell had Liz said to her?

"Please tell me you didn't?" Carly asked from the kitchen doorway.

Turning to face his sister. He had not heard her come over to him, and he knew by the way she was looking at him that he was wearing his emotions on his face. Normally he was a pro at hiding them, but in certain circumstances, when his feelings became too overwhelming, the façade would slip. Normally he was on his own.

This time however his sister was there to catch it.

Chance knew he was busted, but he also knew he could play one of two ways. He could tell her the truth, or he could act like he didn't know what Carly was talking about.

Chance opted for the second option, as he was not in the mood to discuss his feelings.

Especially not with his sister.

So, he tried to ride it.

Turning away from the stairs, Chance walked into the kitchen and poured himself a cup of coffee.

"I have no idea what you are talking about. I simply wanted to know if she was okay. I saw her talking to Liz before I came in." He said innocently, as he took a sip of the sweet brew.

Carly simply shook her head.

"I swear to God, Chance, if I lose the best nanny and best friend I have ever had because you couldn't quit being a man for one second, I will make you pay."

The notion of Paris leaving had never even crossed his mind, and now that it had he was furious. Putting his cup on the counter he turned to face the window so that his sister could not read his features.

"Calm down, you are not going to lose her," Chance growled back, he had tried to make his tone as light as possible, but he still couldn't help the frustration that seeped in.

Chance couldn't blame his sister for her doubts as he was well known for bedding and then leaving women.

But Paris was different.

He couldn't explain why; he just knew it to be so.

Whenever she wasn't around him, he felt empty and the thought of her ever leaving left him with a hurt so deep inside that he wondered if it would ever go away.

Chance suspected he was falling in love with her, but he was not ready to admit that to himself, let alone anyone else.

Chance wanted to deny that there was nothing going on between him and Paris, but at that moment with his emotions running wild, he knew he wouldn't be able to convince anyone, let alone Carly.

So he said nothing.

Turning away from his sister, Chance decided to head up to his bed, a bed that was going to be cold and lonely tonight. He stopped briefly at Paris' door, he raised his hand prepared to knock.

He wanted so badly to go in and make her change her mind about any decision she was planning, but before he could he realised how selfish he was being.

What if she really was sick? He thought; then he would just look like an insensitive clod. So instead of knocking, Chance sighed and made his way over to his own room.

Before he entered, he looked at her door once more. What was one more night going to do; he could wait until the morning to talk to her.

He still had time to make her change her mind.

Walking into his room, Chance showered and climbed into bed.

As he lay there staring at the ceiling, he prayed that come morning everything would be alright.

It wasn't like she would leave in the middle of the night.

Turning over, Chance fell into a restless sleep.

CHAPTER TWENTY-ONE

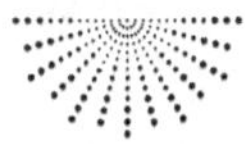

Waking up, Chance stretched before he got out of bed. He couldn't remember the last time he'd slept so badly, he was going to need a lot of coffee this morning before he did anything.

The other thing Chance needed to do was to talk to Paris and that was going to be his first priority.

Getting up and getting dressed, Chance made his way out of his room and across the hall to Paris' door. He knew he should probably wait until she came and found him, but the way she had been acting last night had left him with an uneasy feeling, and he had the sudden urge to see her.

Chance raised his hand to knock on her door, but before he could, common sense prevailed. She was probably already up and downstairs as she usually was.

Turning on his heel Chance made his way down to the kitchen, which he found empty.

That in itself was strange, Carly was usually the first one up.

Chance shrugged, he was kind of glad that he was alone,

it would give him time to get coffeed up and come up with a plan.

Pouring himself a drink, he leaned back against the counter and tried to think of what he was going to say to Paris.

A knocking at the door interrupted his thoughts.

Placing his cup on the counter, Chance walked on bare feet to the door and opened it

He was not sure he was expecting at this hour of the morning, but the three men who stood before him were not it.

"May I help you?" Chance asked the older gentlemen who was in the middle.

He was quite tall, with blonde hair and Chance pegged him as being somewhere in his sixties.

The younger man on his left looked a lot like him, but it was the man on the right that caused Chance the most concern. While the first two men could have passed for businessmen, the one on the right looked like a thug.

"Perhaps." The older man answered.

"Have you seen this girl?" The man on the left asked handing Chance a picture.

At first glance Chance did not have a clue as to who the girl was, but the more he looked at it he came to realise that it was Paris, only with blonde hair.

"You see that is my daughter, she moved here from Australia a few years ago and we only just found out that she has been missing for a few months." The man in the middle added.

Normally Chance would have helped anyone who was looking for their child, but the look that Paris wore last night along with the bad vibe Chance was getting about the men at his door saw him lying through his teeth.

There was no way he was going to tell them that Paris

was here, not until he'd had the chance to talk to her anyway. If she wanted to contact them after that, then he would leave that up to her.

There had to be a reason that she hadn't contacted them before now.

"Sorry but I have never seen this girl before. Maybe you should check in town." Chance offered to make his answer more believable.

"Look again." The thug looking guy snarled shoving the picture at Chance once more.

Chance did not back down. The man's actions only cemented his actions to keep Paris safe.

"It won't help, the only females that are on this Ranch currently is my sister and my niece who is young. So, if you gentlemen wouldn't mind I would like to get back to work."

Chance was just about to shut the door when the thug stepped forward and placed his hand on it, effectively stopping the motion.

Chance was pissed, how *dare* they come here and act as if they could scare him.

"Shall I call the police." He stated pointedly.

The older gentleman seemed to realise his mistake; he placed his hand on the arm of the other man.

The tall brute looked at the old man, and when he nodded, he removed his hand.

"I am sorry for my companion's brashness, we are all just anxious to find Paris. But obviously we have been given the wrong information. We will leave you to your day."

The mention of Paris' name only confirmed Chance's suspicions, and the fact that they did not want the police involved also confirmed that Paris was probably hiding from them.

What mess was she mixed up in? Chance wondered.

He did not try to shut the door again, instead he watched

to make sure the men left. The last thing he wanted was for them to take any more time than they needed and still be here when Paris innocently came down stairs.

The men had just made it to the end of the walk when the older man stopped and faced Chance again.

"I just have one more question if you would indulge me."

The last thing he wanted to do was answer any more questions, but he had a feeling that until he gave them an answer they would not leave.

"Sure." He fired.

"Could you tell us where to find Liz?"

So that was it, this was all Liz's doing. Chance was starting to put the puzzle together; she had obviously seen them the day at the barn and this was her way of getting Paris out of his life.

Well he had news for her, her ploy was not going to work. Even if Paris did have to leave, there was no way Chance would ever be with a woman like her.

"You can find her over at the cattle yards." He supplied to the men, before shutting the door. He didn't even feel a little bad for dumping her lying arse in the frying pan. This was one mess she was not going to get out of so easily.

Chance spun around and rushed through the kitchen, he needed to find Paris and he needed to find her now. They had a lot of talking to do. Then they needed to decide what they were going to do with her, because once the men spoke to Liz, he was sure they would be back, with her in tow.

Chance was just entering the living room when he ran smack right into his sister. He grabbed her shoulders to steady her, before he rushed past her to the stairs.

"Bloody hell Chance, where are you going in such a hurry and who was at the door?"

He didn't have time to stop and fill her in so he simply

answered, "I'll fill you in as soon as I can, right now I have to talk to Paris."

He didn't hang around to hear her reply, he took the rest of the stairs two at a time and when he reached Paris' door he didn't even stop to knock. He simply opened the door and barged in.

"Paris, we need to talk."

Chance had expected to find her still in bed, but when his eyes fell on it and he noticed she was not there, he looked around to find her.

But she was not there.

A foreboding filled Chance. It was not so much what he was seeing, as the room looked as it normally would. It was more about what he was not seeing; there was nothing of Paris left in the room.

This was not good.

Deciding that he could not spend any more time considering what had happened, Chance rushed to his room to collect his keys and wallet. She couldn't have gotten too far, and with those men on the lookout for her too, Paris was in danger and he needed to help her.

Chance was just about out the door when an envelope leaning against the mirror on the duchess caught his attention. He thought about leaving it until he returned, but once again his instincts kicked in telling him he needed to read it.

Picking it up, he saw his name scrawled across the front.

It was Paris handwriting.

This was not good.

Sitting back heavily on his bed, Chance ripped the envelope open, and began to read.

With each line he read, his heart broke and that pit in his stomach that had been present over the last few weeks showed him just how in love he was with Paris.

. . .

Dear Chance,

I want to thank you for showing me that in love there is free-dom. I know that might not make sense to you, as I was the only one stupid enough to go and fall in love, but I couldn't help it. I love you. I love you more than I have loved anyone in my entire life. I am not sure when it happened or how it happened, but it did. And as much as I want it to remain with you and explore this love forever, I can't. It would not be fair to you or your family.

You see over the last few months you and your family have provided me with a dream that I have had my whole life. The dream that I was part of something important and great. And while I would love nothing more than to spend more time with you to see if this dream of mine could become a reality, I can't. If my life has taught me anything over the years it is that life itself is not fair and while I may wish upon every star that what we shared could become a reality, the truth is that all it will ever be is a dream.

Please know that it was never my intention to hurt any of you and know that if I could stay, I would. But I cannot allow my damaged life to ruin you. I love you too much to allow my tarnished soul to ruin the light that shines in yours. You are the light of my days and the moon of my nights. I will forever remember you and I hope in time you find someone who is worthy of all you have to give, and that they make you as happy as you have made me.

Thank you for giving me something to fight for.

Thank you for giving me the chance to love someone as special as you.

You will forever be in my heart.

You will remain my love for eternity.

Please do not try to find me, it will only cause you more pain.

Forever in love,

Paris.

.   .   .

CHANCE'S EYES continued to read and re-read over Paris' words. He had no idea what he was feeling.

Yes he did, anger.

He was not angry at her, he was angry at the fates that had conspired to bring her to him and then take her away.

Screwing up the letter, Chance threw it against the wall.

Chance stood up and started pacing the floor, running his hands through his hair. He had to decide what to do. He could let her go and do as she asked, or he could try and find her and discover what the hell was going on.

He paced for a few more minutes, thinking back over the past few months and when his mind settled on the image of her lying in his arms, her soft eyes smiling up at him, he knew that there was nothing in this world that could keep him from her.

There was no way he was going to let her go.

Now that he knew she loved him as much as he loved her, he had to fight for her.

"Screw this." Chance said out loud. Whatever she thought she is protecting him from, they could work it out together.

There was no way he was letting her get away, and there was no way he was letting her face those goons alone.

With purposeful steps, Chance yanked his door open, and made his way down to the kitchen, he needed a cup of coffee for what needed to be done, and he would have to come up with a plausible explanation for Carly.

He had expected to still find her there, but he had not been expecting the scene he waked into. As he rounded the door he was met with his sister's tears. She was holding a letter of her own, a letter he knew was from Paris, but that was not what worried him the most.

It was the two men sitting at her table that offered him a moment's pause.

"Carly?" he asked.

His sister wasn't given the opportunity to answer him, one of the men hopped up from the table and offered his hand for Chance to shake.

"Good morning, Mr Malloy. I am Detective Johnson, and this is my partner, Detective Gantor. We are sorry to interrupt your morning, but we could sure use your help."

He had a bad feeling that this was connected with the men who had been here this morning, and it only added to the urgency in which he needed to find Paris. But Chance also knew that polite society dictated that he inquire about their business before he rushed out.

"That is quite alright. But may I ask what this early morning visit is about?" Chance asked distractedly, hoping that they would get to whatever it was they needed and fast.

Time was running out.

"Please sir, have a seat, this may take a while. We need to talk to you about Miss Devon. We are hoping that you may be of some assistance in finding her."

Chance gave them a confused look. He was kind of relieved though.

This wasn't about Paris at all.

"I'm sorry detective, but I think you must be mistaken there is no Miss Devon here. Now if you don't mind, I need to get to work."

The detectives looked back down at their notes. Before they looked once more at Chance.

"Look sir, I know this may be confusing. But we have it on good authority that a one Miss Paris Devon had been seen here yesterday."

That last bit caught his attention.

Surly they weren't talking about his Paris?

If so, why were these detectives here for her?

Who was Paris really?

All of these questions were flying around in Chance's

head. He had no answers for any of them, the only thing he did know the answer to was how he felt about her.

He loved her. It was that simple.

The rest would work itself out.

"Do you have a picture of the woman you are looking for?" he asked, wanting to make one-hundred percent sure it was Paris they were talking about.

The detective handed him a photo of the woman they were looking for and his heart froze as he stared into the eyes of the woman he loved.

Chance did not care about why they were looking for her. In truth, there was only one thing he needed to know.

"Is she in some kind of trouble?" He asked, unable to keep the frantic tone out of his voice.

Both of the detectives looked at each other before answering.

"It's hard to say sir. But we are pretty sure that if we don't find her soon, these men just might."

Chance looked down at the table where photos of the three men from this morning lay. Chance's heart beat faster. He knew they were trouble.

He had to find Paris now.

Chance stood up, shook the hands of the detectives and replied, "I would love to help, but if you would…"

But before they could finish, Carly wiped her tears and said, "Chance, if you love her at all, you will sit down and listen to what these two men have to say."

Chance wanted nothing more than to run after Paris and make sure she was okay, he needed to get to her before they did. But the seriousness of his sister's tone and the look on the detectives' faces had him sitting.

He would be of no use to Paris if he did not have all the facts. He had no idea how long she had been gone already, and he was certain that another hour would not make much of a difference.

She had managed to stay on the run this long, he was sure she would survive another hour.

"Alright, what do you need from me?" He asked sitting back down.

And with that, the detectives filled him on everything that had happened, not only a few months ago but years ago as well.

Chance and Carly learned everything they needed to know about who Paris really was.

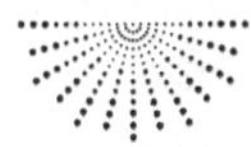

Paris opened the door to the Riverton motel.

She had not gotten as far enough away from Cody as she had liked, in fact, she was just one town over.

Paris had been driving around in circles since this morning, trying to decide what to do.

She had every intention of leaving and getting as far out of dodge as she could, but every time she had ended up on the highway driving away from Cody, she only got a few miles down the road before she turned around and headed back.

She couldn't leave them.

The tears that had kept falling and the emotions of what she'd had to do were taking a toll on her.

It was now close to dark, and she needed to pull over and rest for the night. She was hoping that with a little rest, some clarity and sense would come to her.

The morning would be soon enough to continue on with her journey.

Paris walked in and put her stuff on the spare bed that

was in the room. Looking around she took in the sparse furnishings.

It was far from the Hyatt hotel, but it would do.

Paris sat down on her own bed and contemplated how things had turned out so wrong.

When she had first arrived at Blackridge Ranch, she had only expected to stay a month at the most, and she had promised not to get attached to anyone.

Then Chance had happened.

And while she knew this day would come eventually, Paris had been hoping that she could live in denial for ever and that it never would.

How *stupid* could she have been to think that she could hide forever.

She guessed the jig was up now.

Not only was there was a national manhunt for her, but she also had her family on her tail. Paris was not sure which one she feared the most. Either way she was screwed, she was either going to end up in jail, or forced to return home with a family she wanted nothing to do with.

Paris stood up and walked to the mirror. As she stood there looking at the reflection that was staring back at her, she made a decision.

Come morning she would dye her hair again, forget everything that had happened here, and she would once again go on the run.

Only this time she would have to do a better job of hiding.

Paris turned away from the reflection of the girl she no-longer knew and walked into the bathroom to wash her face.

The bathroom was even worse than the main room. The old chipped tiles looked as though they had come straight out of a 70's slasher film.

Paris took one look at the shower and decided that she could do without one tonight.

Paris couldn't complain really, as the saying went, you got what you paid for, and the good thing about this place it was cheap and she paid in cash; no questions would be asked.

Turning the tap on, Paris splashed some water on her face, trying to remove the mess that her tears had made.

Looking up after the water had been placed there, it she looked even worse than she had moments ago. Black streaks were now running in rivulets down her face, and her eyes were still red and puffy.

Deciding there was not much more she could do, she reached for the towel beside the basin, and after drying her face; Paris made her way over to the bed and picked up her phone.

She hadn't turned it on since she had left Seattle, but she guessed now that the cat was out of the bag, it was as good a time as any to check what was going on.

The moment her iPhone lit up, a message let her know that her memory was full and needed to be cleaned out. She had multiple missed calls and messages from everyone; ranging from the police, her colleagues and college friends, to multiple calls from an unknown number.

Paris opened a few and read them, but the gist was pretty much the same throughout.

All of them wanted to know where she was and what had happened that night in the hotel room with Charmaine.

Some even begged her to give herself up. She wasn't surprised that they thought she had done it.

The message that she had received from Charmaine's parents was her undoing. Tears once more streamed down her face as she read the words over and over.

. . .

Paris Hunny, we have no idea what happened that night, but what we do know without certainty is that you in no way had anything to do with her murder. But in saying that we need to know what happened to our baby. You need to contact the police so that we can put her to rest. If you know what happened to our baby, you owe it to her to come forward. The longer you hide the harder it will be. Please, you are the only one who knows the truth.

Paris threw the phone against the wall. Surly everyone should know that if she knew the truth, then she would have come forward.

Why did everyone feel the need to guilt trip her into doing something? Paris *knew* she owed Charmaine, no-one had to tell her that. With each passing day where Charmaine remained dead and her killer lived his life happily, guilt ate her up inside.

She knew she was letting her best friend down. She just didn't know how to fix it.

Paris threw herself into the pillow and screamed out all of her frustration.

Perhaps it would be best for everyone if she joined Charmaine.

Nobody would truly miss her, and Chance and his family would be safe.

Once the police or her family caught up with her, her life was going to be over anyway. It was just a waiting game now.

The game of seeing who got to her first.

Paris didn't know if she would be able to handle going to jail, but she sure as hell did know that she wouldn't survive going home with her family.

With that thought in mind, Paris chucked on her hoodie, pulled it up over her face and made her way over to the pharmacy not far from where she was staying.

After she had gotten what she wanted, Paris headed back to her hotel and let herself in.

Placing the pills on the table next to the bed, Paris laid

down once more, staring at them trying to decide what to do.

Thoughts of what her life would be like if her family caught her, or if she ended up in jail. The cold empty road lying in front of her for the rest of her life played on repeat in her head, while a tiny voice kept telling her to end it.

Only her love for Chance was stopping her.

With thoughts of him reaching her mind, the tears began to flow again and soon all of the fear, anger, pain and despair she had felt for the past few months carried her off into a fitful sleep.

Paris was back in the room with Charmaine and the two men. Confusion filled her mind, she swore she had just been in a motel alone and for some unknown reason she didn't feel as though she belonged here.

"Here have a drink." The tallest of the two men with dusty brown hair offered her. Her mind was screaming at her not to have it, but for some reason she reached out and took it. Looking over at her friend, she smiled as she watched Charmaine dance and drink with the darker haired of two the men. The man she swore she knew.

Paris smiled at the man and drank her drink in one gulp, it kind of tasted funny, she wanted to spit it out, but no matter how hard she tried to open her mouth, she couldn't. Instead she swallowed it.

Paris was just about to comment on it when she started to sway a bit.

"Whoa, here let's sit down," the man beside her was saying as he gently led her to the couch.

Paris expected him to sit with her, but instead he laid her down, crouched down in front of her and pushed a strand of hair behind her ear before saying, "Now you be a good girl and wait here for your turn."

Paris blinked trying to clear her mind of what that meant, but when she opened them again, she could see them tearing Charmaine's clothes off.

Paris knew she should help her friend, but no matter how hard she tried Paris couldn't move her body and all she could do was watch as her friend was killed.

Tears streamed down her face when the same man who had laid her down on the couch came back over to her.

Picking her up, he placed her on the bed, beside her friend. "I will do the honours this time," the guy who had been with her said to his friend.

"Please...." Paris croaked out.

"Oh yes Hunny, that's it, beg. We love it when they beg." He hissed. Paris blinked when she thought she saw a snake's tongue dart out of his mouth.

Then he ran the knife over her legs and arms, and even though it felt as though her skin was on fire with each cut, Paris could not move. But she did scream. Closing her eyes, she screamed with all she had.

Only when their hands covered her mouth did she stop. She knew what was coming. But she could do nothing to stop it.

"That's enough!" Came the voice of his friend.

The man above her stopped.

He looked furious.

But it was nothing with the look that washed over the eyes of his companion.

His eyes held no colour, no life, no soul.

Paris swore he was the devil himself.

She could see that the man who was above her wanted to continue, but he was more afraid of his companion, so instead of killing her, he leaned forward, and ran his tongue the length of her face.

"Oh, how I would love to have more of you." He whispered into her ear before he stuck his tongue in her ear.

"I said enough." His partner bellowed.

The man above her removed his tongue. His head slowly came back so that he was now staring straight in her eyes. The look she saw then told her that if he could, he would end her life the way he had Charmaine's.

He got off on it.

Paris held her breath waiting to see what he would do, she would have given anything to be able to move. She did not let go of the breath she was holding, until he got off the bed and handed his partner the knife.

"You are one lucky bitch." He replied before they headed for the door.

Paris could only watch as they removed any evidence that they had been here, before they made their way out. She had expected them to just leave, but when the darker of the two stopped at the door, giving her an evil smile, she thought her life was over.

"Good luck getting out of this." He commented cryptically. Paris could have sworn he wanted to say something else.

"Ivan, we have to go." His friend said returning to the door.

Paris was not sure what happened next as their voices became muffled as he closed the door and left her to her fate.

That was the last thing Paris remembered before the drugs finally took over and she passed out.

CHAPTER TWENTY-THREE

Paris awoke in the motel screaming. As she looked around the room, she noticed the sun was setting, and the shadows in the room added to the haunting feeling she had from her nightmare.

Finally, it had all come rushing back. The fog of confusion had cleared and showed the reality of what had really happened that night. The false memories were replaced with the real ones.

Paris finally knew who was behind this whole damn mess. She knew she had known the guy from the bar somewhere, but it wasn't until she remembered hearing his name that Paris knew.

Her father was behind this whole damn mess.

Paris got out of bed and started pacing as everything started to make sense.

The note on the mirror.

The reason she was left alive.

It all came down to her father.

Ivan was her father's henchman who handled the stuff that was too dirty for her father to handle. He was the one who got his hands dirty as such.

Ivan must have been the one who had hired the guy who murdered her friend. It was no wonder it took all this time for Paris to remember, she had only ever seen Ivan a few times, and she had been much younger.

Paris continued to pace back and forth trying to think about what her next move would be. She had to go to the police with what she knew. But she also needed proof of what she was saying.

Paris sat on her bed, resting her head in her hands trying to think of what to do.

Then it hit her.

That night at the bar, she and Charmaine had been taking selfies of each other. She would still have those photos on her phone. Maybe just maybe one of them caught Ivan and his friend there.

Paris quickly made her way over to where her phone still lay on the floor from the night before.

"Come on baby please work." She whispered as she turned it on.

Due to Paris' frustrated, angry outburst the day before, the screen was cracked right through, but thankfully it still turned on.

As Paris unlocked the phone, and the home screen came on her finger lightly brushed over the phone icon. Maybe she should get Carly's number and call Chance, he would know what to do.

But the moment the crossed her mind, it was gone just a quick. She had to deal with this on her own, she could not and would not put him in anymore danger than she had done already.

Her father was here to take her home, she knew it in her bones. And considering that he had killed her best friend in order to, so it also meant that nothing and no-one she loved was safe.

Chance and his family were better off with her far away from them.

Paris forgot about ringing anyone, instead she opened her photo albums and started to flick through the photos from that night.

With each one that showed Charmaine's smiling face tears began to flow. But then, she found the photo she wanted.

The photo was one of Charmaine turned, waving at a guy. Although it appeared as though she was shooting her friend, Paris had in fact been shooting the guy, at the behest of her friend, so the photo was focused on the bar.

But it was not the guy Charmaine was waving too that caught Paris' eye, it was the two men just off to his right, who were intently staring at her.

It was Ivan and his buddy.

Paris wiped the tears from her eyes and got to her feet.

"We've got them Char," she whispered to herself.

Now all she had to do was go to the police.

Paris tried to turn the television on. She was hoping she would find a newscast that was still appealing to people for her whereabouts. She wanted to get the number to the detective who was on the case. She wanted to go straight to the top with the information she had.

But as luck would have it the television was not working. Paris decided to go to the front counter and see if there was a computer she could use.

Paris opened the door and was just about to walk out when she noticed three men walking past her.

It took her a minute to register, but when she did, she stepped back into her room and slammed the door.

Her father was here.

What the hell was she going to do?

She silently prayed that they hadn't seen her, but she knew that was wishful thinking, because before she had shut the door, she locked eyes with her brother.

Oh God they were both here.

Paris looked around the room for something she could use as a weapon, but there was nothing.

Paris looked at the door wondering how long it would take them to come in.

Noticing the door was not locked, she quickly ran forward and turned the deadbolt, before putting the chain on it as well.

She leaned her head against the door trying to slow her heart rate.

A small rap came thought the door to greet her ears.

"Well well well, if the little birdy didn't just fall into our laps. Come on Paris open the door. Don't make us do anything stupid." Her brother said through the door in a singsong voice.

She hated that voice. He had used it on her all the time as kid. It was his way of making her feel stupid.

"Why can't you just leave me alone." She asked.

She had expected her brother to answer again. This time it was her father.

"Because dear child. You are part of our family, and you disgraced our family when you left. Now it is time for you to come home and make it up to us. Now stop being a brat and open the door."

Paris jumped back when his fist slammed into the door.

Walking backwards, Paris knew it would only be a few minutes more before they were in. She was sure Ivan would break down the door if he had to.

Paris had to think quick. She needed evidence of their wrong doing, but the only thing she had on her was her phone. If they found it on her they would take it.

But she needed it for proof.

Paris looked around the room and as her eyes landed on the small bench in front of the mirror, she had a brainwave.

Opening her bag, she opened the first aid kit she always carried on her. Then turning her phone to silent so it didn't ring, she turned on the app that would start recording. From previous times she had used the app she knew she had about twenty minutes record time.

But as she hit it, her phone reminded her that the memory was full.

Paris almost dropped the phone when the first loud bang came through the door. She had to hurry.

Paris opened her messages and quickly deleted them all, punching in Carly's number she sent her quick message telling her where she was, before she once again hit the record button.

Once she was sure it was recording Paris used all the tape, she had to stick the phone to the underside of the table. She didn't have time to check her handy work, she just had to pray that this worked.

If it didn't, she was screwed anyway.

Paris had just gotten to her feet and was near the bed when the door burst open.

She wanted to cower away when her father walked in, but she wouldn't. She was not going to let him know how much she feared him.

So she stood her ground.

She stood her ground as he walked up to her.

She stood her ground as her brother and Ivan checked that she was alone.

She stood her ground as her father backhanded her.

She had already given him enough tears; she would not shed anymore.

"Why?" she asked.

Her father turned his back on her and took in the room.

"Why what?" he finally asked turning back to her.

"Why did you kill my friend?"

Her father's eyes narrowed. He was a man who never gave anything away. And now that he was standing in front of her once more, she was reminded of what a cold man he was.

He had never loved her.

And she knew that now, especially after she'd experienced real love.

"What makes you think I had anything to do with it?" He asked, a sly smile playing on his lips.

Her father was a master at talking his way around things. She knew that if she wanted to take him down along with Ivan, she had to get him to admit his part in the murder.

Paris pointed to Ivan as he came out of the bathroom.

"He was there that night. And he only does things at your behest."

Her father looked at Ivan, laughter in his eyes.

"So, it all finally came back to you did it Sweetheart?" Ivan asked in an evil sneer.

Paris had wondered if the evil she'd witnessed in him that night was due to the drugs, or if it was really him.

She now had her answer.

"Well there is no use denying it any further. The truth of the matter is, *you* are the reason she is dead dear girl. If you hadn't run, then we wouldn't have followed. And once we did follow, we knew the only way to get you home would be to take away your life here."

Her father's words sickened her. He had outstretched his arms to make his point.

"And that is exactly what I did." Ivan continued.

Paris wanted to scream at them. Charmaine had lost her life, just because her father wanted to ruin hers.

"I will not go willingly." Paris added as she backed away from the three men.

"We thought you might say that."

Her brother answered walking towards her, with a rope in his hand.

Paris started to panic a new.

"You can tie me up, gag me or even carry me over your shoulder. But know this. I will make such a scene that it *will* draw attention. I know someone in this town will call the cops.

Her brother stopped at her words. There was glimmer of hope. That was until Ivan spoke again.

"Don't worry boss. I will simply make more of the drug we used that night. It will knock her out and then we can get her home with no fuss."

Paris knew her father would have flown here on a private jet, so she knew once they knocked her out the game was over.

Her only hope of being saved lay in Chance's hands.

"Okay, you go get the stuff. Tommy, tie your sister up good and then go and find us another car. While you are doing that, I am going to go and make our arrangements and get some decent food."

Paris started to struggle and scream when Ivan grabbed her and placed her on the only chair in the room.

She continued to scream as her arms were roughly pulled behind her back where they were tied so tight, they were cutting of the circulation.

"And for God sake shut her up." Her father's harsh tone echoed as he left the room.

Paris' screams were cut off when Tommy ripped off a piece of his shirt and placed it over her mouth. He pulled it so tight that it cut into the sides of her lips, she was lucky she could breath.

He then walked to the front of her and slapped her face. "We will see ya soon, Sis, don't go anywhere."

He was laughing at his own joke when he and Ivan walked out the door shutting it as they went.

Paris tried to move her hands and scream, but it was to no avail.

She was trapped.

Tears began to run down her face once more.

Please God let someone find me.

CHAPTER TWENTY-FOUR

"**P**aris, I know you are in there. Open the door."

Chance's voice came through to her.

Was he really here?

Paris wanted to scream out to him, but the gag that was still in her mouth cut of any sound she could make.

Paris started stamping her feet, hoping that the noise would be heard through the door. It must have worked because the next thing she knew, he was busting through the door. There wasn't much of a door left, so it didn't take much to open.

Paris could sit there and look at him as he stood there larger than life.

He had come.

He was wearing his typical country get up, he was breathing hard, and the moment his eyes rested on her, there was a mix of relief and anger.

This stuff only happened in the movies, she thought as he rushed forward to remove the binding on her mouth and hands.

She wanted to tell him how much she loved him, and she

wanted him to take her in his arms and hold her tight. But she still wasn't sure what he knew or how he felt about her, so the only thing she could thing to say was, "You are probably going to have to pay for that door, you know?"

Chance was not amused by her attempt at humour.

He ran his hands over her body, "are you hurt anywhere?" he asked.

Paris was just about to answer him when two other men entered the room. She had no idea who they were, but she knew *what* they were.

"I can explain everything I promise. I didn't kill her. I swear." Paris was rambling as she ran to the table, squatted down and removed her phone.

She then walked up to the detective and handed him the phone. "All the proof you need of who killed Charmaine is on there." She explained.

No-one seemed in a hurry to move. Paris was starting to worry.

Why weren't they doing anything?

Her father and his posse would be back any minute now.

Paris had to do something. She grabbed Chance's shirt and pleaded with him between gasps. "You have to believe me. I didn't do it. There is no way I could kill her. But I finally know who did. You have to believe me. It's all there on the phone. Please Chance you have to believe me."

Paris could feel herself getting hysterical, so she was surprised when Chance pulled her into his arms and started to rub circles on her back.

"Paris, calm down, sweetheart. We know you didn't do it. These detectives have been trying to find you to let you know they know who did it."

Paris looked at Chance in confusion. "What? They know?" Chance wasn't given the opportunity to answer her.

The taller of the two detectives looked at Paris and confirmed, "Yes, that is right, Miss Michaels, we know."

Paris gasped at the use of her real name.

She removed herself from Chance's arms and went and sat on the bed.

She put her head in her hands.

"So that means you know who I really am."

She looked up in time to see the detective nod.

"Yes, we do. But if you wouldn't mind, we would like for you to come down to the local police station and tell us everything you know."

Shocked, Paris simply nodded before she turned back to Chance. "I'm so sorry I didn't tell you what was going on, but I didn't know how to. And then when I heard Liz on the phone to my father along with the newscast that showed him looking for me, I panicked. I am so sorry; I hope you can forgive me. I understand if you don't."

Paris was afraid that the only reason Chance had come with the detectives was to make sure they got her.

But, he sat down beside her and when he placed his hand under her chin and lifted it to meet his eyes; she was once again filled with hope, hope that this was all going to work out.

"Sweetheart, don't worry about all that now, we can talk about that later. For now, let's get you down to the station so you can give your statement."

Paris' heart filled with joy when Chance leant down and kissed her.

But just as that joy filled her heart, it was replaced with terror.

Her father was still here. And he would be back any minute. So far, her father didn't know anything about Chance, and she wanted to keep it that way.

"You have to go." She said standing and trying to drag him to the door.

"Paris what are you going on…"

"Please Chance just go, they will be back soon."

Paris couldn't understand why nobody was listening to her.

"Paris." Chance coxed as he removed her hand form his arm.

"Explain." Paris looked deep into his eyes and then threw her hands up in the air. She knew she wasn't going to budge him until he had the answers he wanted.

She started pacing the floor and filled both Chance and the detective in on what had been happening before they arrived. When she had finished, she had expected them to both leave, but they didn't.

"This could work in our favour." The first detective said to his partner.

"Yes. If we leave now we lose our chance at finally capturing this arsehole." The other one said.

"What exactly are you two suggesting?" Chance asked jumping into their foray.

"Simply put Mr Malloy, we want to use your girlfriend as bait."

Paris hand covered her mouth as squeak escaped.

Chance gave her a knowing look. "What do you say sweetheart? How about we finally put this scum away?"

Paris was shaking her head. She knew what they were asking her, but she didn't know if she could.

It wasn't that she felt anything for her family; it was more that she was scared of what they would do if they all failed.

Paris was shaking her head vehemently, "No, no it is not going to happen." She had once again gone back to pacing the room.

Chance grabbed her arm and stopped her in front of him.

But his charms were not going to work this time. There was no way she was going to willingly put him in danger.

"What are you afraid of?" He asked her softly.

Tears began to fall. She didn't know if she had the strength to tell him all of it.

"Paris?" Looking up into his eyes, she knew she was lost.

"I am afraid of losing you, as I lost Charmaine. Her death tore me apart, but if anything happened to you, I would not survive. I love you Chance." The tears were falling in earnest now, "so please, just go and live your life."

She went to pull away from him, but he grabbed her once more and pulled her back.

"I am not going anywhere. How could I leave the woman I love to face the monsters of her past?"

Paris' eyes flew to his.

She wasn't sure she understood what he was saying.

"You love me. Are you sure?"

Chance laughed. "Only you would ask me that. Yes, I love you and if you think I am about to lose you again you are sorely mistaken. Now what do you say we stop these monsters so that we can go home and start out lives together."

"Home?" Paris questioned.

"Yes home, because there is no way you are leaving me again."

Paris heart filled to the brim with love for this man. He was right, she could not let her father get away with the crimes he had committed anymore.

Turning to the detective she placed her hand in Chance's before saying, "okay what is the plan?"

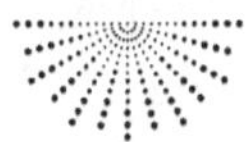

CHAPTER TWENTY-FIVE

"What on earth made you decide to steal a minivan?" Paris braced herself for the confrontation she knew was about to occur.

Chance was currently hiding in the shower; while the two detectives had moved to the room next door. They wanted to make sure that their cover wasn't blown on top of being near enough to save Paris.

She had begged Chance to go with them, but he was adamant on staying close by.

While a part of her was scared for his welfare, the other part was thankful for his presence.

She turned her head so she could see into the bathroom, Chance winked at her and mouthed 'show time' before he placed himself behind the half-closed door.

Paris was almost certain that her father would not re-check the room, as they had no reason to suspect foul play.

"Hey, it will be easier to hide a drugged body in minivan." Tommy defended his actions as him and Ivan walked through the door.

"Idiot." Ivan mumbled as he shoved past Tommy and made his way over to the bench.

"It was nice of you to wait for us." Tommy laughed as he walked past Paris, kicking her feet as he did.

He then threw himself on the bed, crossing his feet at the ankles and placing his hands behind his head, he continued to chuckle to himself over his joke.

Paris had been re-tied up in order to set the trap. They wanted Paris' father to think as though he had gotten away with everything.

"Why don't you make yourself useful and get me some water." Ivan growled at Tommy from where he had continued to unpack his items.

"And what the hell am I supposed to put it in?" Tommy asked as he sat up on the bed.

Ivan didn't even bother looking at Tommy as he threw him the glass.

Tommy caught it and headed for the bathroom.

Paris' eyes shot wide with fear as she watched her brother stroll past the door to the sink in the bathroom. She held her breath waiting for the moment Chance would be discovered.

Thankfully her father chose that moment to enter the room.

"Right everything is set. Have you made the mixture yet?" He asked Ivan.

"Just waiting on the water." He replied.

That comment and his father's not so patient 'hurry up', saw Tommy rushing out of the bathroom with the said water.

Paris relaxed a little, but only little; there was still a chance this could all go wrong.

She knew that the detectives were listening through a wire they had attached to her. They were simply waiting for the right moment to bust in.

They had enough evidence to convict her father and his goons, but they wanted to make sure none of them got off on a technicality.

"It's done." Ivan announced as he turned and made his way over to Paris.

Tommy had walked behind her and was undoing her gag.

She needed to get this over quickly.

She started screaming at them all, yelling about how they were all going to pay, and how they wouldn't get away with this.

Tommy grabbed her head and held it still, but before Ivan made it to her, her father walked forward and placed his hands on her chair.

"Now listen here, daughter mine. We will get away with this mark my words. And just know that when I get home, I plan to put you straight to work conning Mr Davenport out of all his hard-earned money, even if you have to whore yourself out. Then I you will spend the rest of your life making up the money you lost me that night you left."

Paris knew that the detectives had just gotten what the needed, now they could also try him internationally for the cons they had only suspected him of.

As it turned out, her father had been on a watch list for years, and only now did they have enough evidence to convict him.

That knowledge gave Paris a freedom she had never felt before, and before she could stop herself, she let loose and spit in her father's face.

She had expected him to backhand her, instead he smiled an evil smile before saying.

"About time you acted like a Michaels." Paris wasn't given the chance to reply, he moved out of the way before saying to Ivan, "now."

Ivan walked forward holding the drug mixture in his

hand, "do you want to do this the easy way or hard way?" he asked.

"Go to hell." Paris spat.

"Hard way it is. Tommy hold her had back and close off her nose." Paris tried to fight him as Tommy did was Ivan asked. She didn't hold out long before her mouth opened of its own accord.

She prayed that something would happen soon to stop this. Just as the thought crossed her mind the two detectives burst through the door.

"Everyone freeze!"

Tommy let go of her head and backed up, while Ivan slowly walked back over to the table.

"You get over here and put your hands against the wall." One of the detectives ordered Tommy.

"Gentlemen. I am not quite sure what you think is going on here, but I have come to take home my drug addicted daughter. She needs help and her family is the only one who can provide it."

Paris snorted as her father tried to con his way out of this situation. She had to give him credit, he was quite the charmer when he wanted to be; it was how he had been so successful for so long.

But this time she had him.

"Quit it Michaels. We don't want to hear it. We know exactly what is going on here and we also know that you are finally going down for all of your crimes; including the death of Miss Charmaine Cole."

For the first time in her life she saw the colour leave her father's face. He knew he was done. But she also knew he would not go down without a fight.

Unfortunately for them, all of the focus had been on Tommy and her father; no-one had been watching Ivan.

He had somehow gotten a gun and now had it pointed at Paris' head.

He untied her from the chair and slowly lifted her out of it, then started walking her around the edge of the room towards the door.

Her father looked at the detective with a smug smile.

"Well Detective, I think we have the upper hand here. So, if you don't mind, I would really love to be getting my daughter home."

Paris was trying to remain calm, but the closer Ivan got her to the door the more she started to panic.

Where was Chance?

Just as if her mind had conjured him, Ivan fell to the ground, limp, behind her. When she spun around, there stood Chance with the copper towel rack in his hand.

He had knocked Ivan out cold.

Paris quickly placed herself behind Chance's back as he picked up the gun and turned it on her father. Now they had three guns trained on them and no hostage.

"I think it is about time you gave up, don't you?" Chance asked cockily.

Her father's calm visage was now gone, as the detectives moved forward to handcuff him.

"You are going to pay for this you bitch." He screamed as the detectives dragged him and her brother out of the hotel room. Once they were in the police car, they came back for Ivan.

Paris was still in shock that it was over, as she watched them cart Ivan off as well.

Once the room was empty of all but her and Chance, he held her close for what seemed like hours, but was only minutes.

She could fell his heart racing through his chest.

"Do you know how hard it was to watch them do that to

you and not be able to stop it?" Chance asked as his shaky hands ran down her back.

Tears started to flow in streams down her face.

"Yes I do, it was how I felt the night they murdered my friend."

As the words left her mouth she could no longer hold it in. Chance lifted her up and carried her to the bed where he just held her and comforted her.

When her tears had subsided, she wiped her face and looked into the eyes of the man she loved.

She had so much to make up to him, she just hoped that when all was said and done he would still love her.

"I am sorry I lied to you. I never meant to hurt any of you, I just didn't know how to…" Paris was finding it hard to put into words what she had been feeling.

But she didn't have too.

Chance shushed her.

"Would you mind sharing it with me now?" he asked. Paris hesitated, worried that by telling him everything it would change how he felt, but the moment she looked into his eyes she somehow knew everything would work out.

"I would like that." She said leaning back into his chest.

And that was how they spent the next hour, cuddled up on a decrepit bed, in a run-down motel while Paris opened up about her life. They then headed down to the police station where she finally gave the statement that would see her father and brother rot for what they did.

CHAPTER TWENTY-SIX

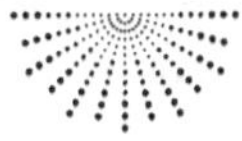

S ix months later….

As Paris sat outside the courthouse in Seattle, waiting to give her testimony against her father and Ivan, her heart began to race. This was going to be the first time since that dreadful night in the hotel room that she was going to come face to face with the monsters who had tried to ruin her life, killed her friend and had almost killed *her*.

The details that Paris remembered from that night, along with the confessions and inside details she knew of her father's shady undertakings were enough to send the lot of them to a dark, dank cell where they could all rot in hell.

When Paris had finally gotten down to the station, the detectives had filled her in on what they had learnt of the night after Charmaine had been killed.

It turned out that the man Ivan had hired to kill Charmaine had unfortunately succeeded in killing two other women in the weeks prior. His MO had been the same as it had been the night, he had been hired to kill her best friend and torture Paris.

If it hadn't been the witness who had seen him with the girls the night of their deaths, he would have gotten away with it. Although Paris wasn't sure about that. She was sure that Ivan would have given up his name eventually.

It also came out in the investigation that he was also linked to five other murders up and down the West Coast. He was going to be lucky if he didn't get a lethal injection as it was still legal in some parts of the States. Thankfully Paris did not have to testify against him as they had enough evidence without her testimony. She did however have to pick him out of a line up.

The moment she saw his sadistic smile as he stood in a line-up of criminals it came rushing back. She knew without a doubt that she would never forget that look.

Paris was brought back to the present when the bailiff opened the door and announced, "five minutes."

Paris' legs started to shake. She didn't know if she could face those monsters again. Since the night she had helped the detectives catch her father and Ivan, she had been waiting for the other shoe to drop; so when the police had told her that her brother had been let out on bail, as they could not hold him for any crime committed in the States, yet, Paris had been scared he would try and find her to shut her up.

She had even considered not testifying.

"They have enough evidence to conflict them without me." She remembered arguing with Carly and Chance one night.

"You're right Sweetheart they do. And no-one will think any less of you if you chose not to testify." Chance had offered pulling her into his arms.

Paris remembered watching Carly as she swirled her drink around in the glass.

"Carly?" She asked.

After the night in the hotel, Paris had gone back to Black-ridge Ranch and told Carly everything. She had expected her friend to hate her, but it had been the opposite; their friendship had only grown stronger, and that was why she waited on her opinion in that moment.

Carly looked up from her glass, shaking her head to remove her thoughts.

"Oh I totally agree with Chance, if you don't want to do it, then you have every right to say no."

"But?" Paris added knowing that Carly was about to say something sensible.

Carly simply smiled at her, "But, you are the only voice Charmaine has, and I still remember how much pain you were in that night you told me about her. I think you need to do this for closure, for her and yourself."

It only took a few more moments of thinking about what Carly had said before Paris decided that she was right. This was not about what Paris wanted; it was about what she needed to do for her friend.

Paris had made her a promise and she was going to keep it.

That wasn't to say that she wasn't terrified.

For the six months, Paris had continued to wake in the middle of the night suffering from night terrors.

Only this time it was different from the months before, Chance had been there to hold her. He sat with her on the window seat looking out over the Wyoming plains, and the star-studded skies, listening to her fears and she finally felt like she was home. This ranch and this cowboy had been her one last chance at freedom, love and safety. Out of all this mess, Paris could be thankful for that.

"Sweetheart, you have nothing to be worried about. I will be with you the whole time and I promise on my life no-one is ever going to hurt you again." Chance said beside her, placing his hand on her leg, bringing her back to the present.

Paris looked at him and smiled; his presence alone and those words were enough to calm Paris. She was not in this alone.

How did she get to be so lucky?

Turning, she grabbed Chance's face and kissed him hard and passionately.

"Thank you for being my rock," she whispered.

"Anytime, Sweetheart." He answered kissing her back. The kiss was soft and sweet, and not enough. Paris was just about to kiss him again, only this time deeper, when the doors to the courtroom opened.

"Miss Michaels, they are ready for you," The court guard announced.

This was it. Standing, she straightened her dress, squared her shoulders and prepared to face the wolves.

"You ready?" Chance asked.

Paris thought about that for moment and then she realised she truly was.

She was ready to put the past behind her and start her future.

She was ready to give Charmaine's family the closure they needed.

She'd had enough of putting her life on hold; it was time to take it back.

Paris couldn't wait to start her new job at the primary school in Cody. And she couldn't wait to see where her relationship with Chance ended up. But first she had to do this one final thing.

"You bet your arse I am, Cowboy." She said and winked.

Chance burst out laughing as they turned and walked into the courtroom. And, with the resounding thud of the courtroom doors closing, Paris knew everything was going to be okay as long as she had Chance, she had hope.

The case had been a closed book. The jury listened to her testimony and that of the other witness, and after only twenty minutes they came back with a guilty verdict.

Paris walked out of the courtroom with a sense of freedom she had never felt before.

It was truly over.

Her life was her own once more.

"Ready to go home?" Chance asked her, pulling her close.

"You bet I am." She answered pulling his arm behind her back with hers. She leaned in and kissed him, before they started to walk to the door.

They were almost there when Detective Johnson called out to them.

"Chance, Paris wait up." He called as he jogged down the hall.

Paris offered him a smile when he reached them.

"I would just like to say thank you again for all of your help." He said smiling back at her.

"It was nothing." She answered shyly.

Chance and Detective Johnson both looked at her as though she had lost her mind.

"Okay it was not nothing, but it was certainly my pleasure." She reiterated.

Both Chance and Detective Johnson laughed. Then the detective looked at Chance.

"Would you mind if I had quick word with Paris." He asked.

Chance nodded before giving her a kiss.

"I will wait just outside the door."

Paris nodded, but as soon as he was out of sight, she felt bereft without his warmth. He had become such an integral part of her life that she missed him when he wasn't there.

Paris stared at the door a bit longer, using her hands to rub her arms, hoping to put some warmth back in them.

"I won't keep you long." The detective started, "I just wanted to give you this. I wasn't sure if you wanted Chance to know."

Paris looked quizzically at the large envelope the detective had handed her, but before she could ask him anything he added.

"You were right about your gut feeling. I hope this helps Chance out of his pickle." He offered her another smile before he turned and started to walk away.

Paris gingerly opened the envelope and pulled out the photos inside. What she found there made her day.

"Thank you." She called out to the detective.

"The pleasure was mine." He called back, waving a hand in the air as he continued to walk.

Paris just shook her head, replaced the photos and headed out to meet Chance.

She couldn't wait to get home and share her news with Carly and him.

EPILOGUE

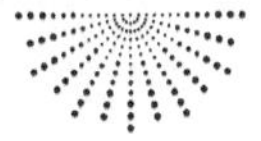

The three of them sat at the table waiting for Liz and her father to show up.

The moment she had shown Chance and Carly the photos that the detective had acquired of Liz in various notorious deeds, some of which included sleeping with many of the rich ranchers as well as stealing money from her own father, they had formed a plan.

Liz was still trying to claim that Chance had promised to marry her; she had even gone so far as to say she was pregnant when Chance returned with Paris.

Since then Liz had been trying to ruin their lives every opportunity she got.

Paris leaned against the bench and smiled into her coffee when the she heard a car pull up. Shit was about to get real.

As she heard the footsteps head up the stairs, Paris put her drink on the bench and prepared to leave.

"I should go and see about the kids and leave you to this." She offered. She didn't want to go anywhere, but this situation really didn't have anything to do with her.

"Don't you *dare* go anywhere." Chance said as he stood up and pulled her into his kiss.

That was how Carly, Liz and her father found them.

"Have you no shame?" Liz's father asked Chance as he pulled the chair out from the table with angry motions.

Chance winked at Paris before he turned around just in time to see Liz sit down at the table and shoot Paris an evil look.

She really was a piece of work, Paris thought. As she stood there watching them, Paris wondered what made Liz become the woman she was today. It had to have been something pretty bad, because even with all of the bad influences that had been in Paris life, and all of the tragedies she had endured, Paris could never allow her pride to sink as low as Liz's was.

"Well Sir, considering this is my house, no I don't."

"What are you going to do young lady, when it turns out my sweet daughter has been telling you the truth this whole time and it turns out Chance has only been using you as he used my Liz?" The man shot at Paris.

Paris simply smiled. "I guess we will never know."

"You will be sorry." Liz snarled.

"I think you will be sorry." Paris bit back. She knew she shouldn't, but the woman was making her mad. She was going to stop but the smug look Liz gave her pissed her off.

"Tell me something Liz, how low does your self-esteem have to be for you to lie about being pregnant?"

Paris wanted to slap Liz's smug face when she leaned back in her chair and smirked.

"It's not a lie. Ask my father. He saw the sonagram, and since Chance is the only man I have been with in the last six months, there is no denying it is his."

The woman was out of her ever-loving mind.

"I haven't touched you in over a year Liz and you know it."

"Why do you keep lying?" Liz was mad once more, she was now standing with her hand on the table and her eyes were shooting daggers at Chance.

"Liz let me handle this." Her father hissed, placing his hand on her arm and effectively shutting his daughter up.

Paris knew it was wrong to feel the glee she felt, knowing that she was about to watch Liz's lies go up in flames, but for reasons that were justified, Paris couldn't dredge up even the smallest amount of pity.

Liz had dug her own grave.

"Now that we have determined that there is no way out of this situation, and that Chance is the only possible candidate to be this baby's father, it is time for me to list my demands. The first thing that will happen is…" Liz's father started.

He was cut off effectively however, when Carly placed the orange A4 envelope in front of the man.

Paris, Chance and Carly didn't say another word; they simply sat there waiting for the fireworks to start.

"What? Is this another one of your tricks?" Liz asked as she squirmed in her seat.

No-one answered her, they simply watched as her father opened the envelope and pulled out the photos that would prove his daughter to be the liar she was.

"Father?" She asked when he still sat quietly and continued to look through the photos.

"Why aren't you…?"

But she never got to say anything else. Her father stood up at the table, and practically threw the photos down in front of her.

She slowly picked them up, shock and terror washed over her face and Paris couldn't wait to see how she tried to back pedal out of this one.

"Father, this is a trick, they have somehow managed to …."

"Shut up, Liz." He roared. "I have had enough of your lying. I told you what was going to happen if I found out you had tried to pull this crap again. You are out of my house."

"Father please." But Liz's words were lost on the man. Paris walked into Chance's arms as the man turned to face them.

"I am truly sorry for any trouble my daughter has caused you Chance. I will make sure that all of your debts and stoppages are lifted first thing and you will be all set to bring your cattle to the yards this year. I will even wave any fees for the term of our contract."

"Thank you Bruce." Chance replied as he shook Liz's father's hand.

"No; thank you for understanding. Now if you wouldn't mind, I would like to get home and start the preparations I need to make for my daughter's travels. Liz lets go."

Liz was sitting at the table, just staring. There were no tears or anything. It seemed to Paris as though she was in shock. She had truly expected a different outcome from this meeting.

Paris wondered briefly if perhaps Liz had become so adapt at lying that she was even starting to believe them herself.

"Bruce, before you go, I have one more thing I would like to do before you leave. I would like you to watch so that you can pass it on to everyone you know so there will be no mistakes like this in the future."

Bruce nodded his agreement.

Paris had no idea what Chance was talking about and she too turned to watch what he was going to do. She had expected him to pull out a contract for Bruce to sign or something, but when he kneeled down in front of her and produced the most gorgeous antique engagement ring she had ever seen, Paris almost fainted.

She needed to grab hold of the chair next to her to keep herself from falling.

Carly was watching on with tears in her eyes.

Could this really be happening?

"Paris, I knew from the moment I ran into you outside of my bedroom door all those months ago that you were different. And while I didn't realise how much of a difference you would make in my life in that moment, it didn't take me long to work it out.

You Paris are the love of my life, and you are the first woman to see past the money and status to see me, and for that I will always be grateful. So, will you do me the honour of being my wife, so that I can spend the rest of my life showing you how much you mean to me?"

Paris was at a loss for words, all she could do was nod.

Chance rose from his place on the ground and placed the ring on her finger. He then pulled her into a passionate kiss.

Carly was the next to hug her, and somewhere in the midst of all the happy laughter and tears, Liz and her father left.

True to his word, Bruce sent Liz off to live with her mother, and he let everyone know that Chance was off the market and happily in love.

"Now that my love life is on track, it is time to make you happy." Paris commented to Carly one night as they sat outside drinking and planning the wedding.

Paris looked up from the magazine she was reading when Carly didn't answer. "Earth to Carly!" she tried once more.

That gained her attention. "Huh, sorry did you say something." Carly asked all flustered.

Paris closely at her friend and noticed that a small blush was rising on her cheeks.

Something was going on.

Following the path to where Carly had been looking moments before, she was just in time to see Bronx putting his shirt back on, he had just finished washing up after being in the barn.

Paris looked back towards her friend with wide eyes.

"Is there something I should know?" Paris asked, laughing when Carly's cheeks got brighter.

"Well I guess you are already on it." Paris added.

Carly threw a piece of fruit at her, "it's not funny." She hissed.

"Do you have something to tell me?" Paris asked in a low whisper, trying to act all secretive.

"What are you two whispering about over here?"

Chance asked as he walked up the stairs to join them Bronx in tow.

Paris sneaked a peak at Carly who seemed to be squirming in her chair, and one look at Bronx only confirmed what she had a sneaking suspicion was a romance in the making.

Paris stood up and walked into Chance's arms. "Oh nothing, just wedding stuff, you know the girly stuff you hate." She offered kissing him on the cheek.

When she turned and looked at Carly once more, the daggers she was shooting her made Paris laugh.

Paris was happy to let the conversation go for now because Paris knew that she would have plenty more opportunities to get the truth out of her sister-in-law.

And that was exactly what she would do. Paris had found her one final chance at love and freedom, and she was determined Carly get hers as well.

Paris wanted everyone to be as happy as she was, everyone deserved that especially Carly.

It was her turn to have her broken heart mended.

www.ingramcontent.com/pod-product-compliance
Lightning Source LLC
Chambersburg PA
CBHW020143120726
47903CB00007B/2392